MW01440816

Copyright © [22023] by [Derek Roberts]

All rights reserved.

No portion of this book may be reproduced in any form without written permission from the publisher or author, except as permitted by U.S. copyright law.

Book Cover Design by K. Sparling

Contents

Forward		IV
Prologue		VI
1.	Waiting for Santa	1
2.	The Most Sadful-est Time of The Year	8
3.	July 4th	15
4.	Leaving Me Here on My Own	22
5.	Believing	30
6.	The Magic of Christmas	37
7.	Little Snowy White Lies	44
8.	$15.82	53
9.	Dinner is Served	61
10.	If Money Grew on Christmas Trees	66
11.	The Sweetest Present	80
12.	Unwrapping the Truth	84
13.	Candy Cane Ville	96
14.	Stars	108
A Note from the Author		123

Forward

Illustration by Lucy Anne Richardson

Dear Cherished Friends of the Festive Season,

It is with boundless joy and a twinkle in my eye that I extend a warm invitation into the enchanting world crafted by Decka. As I, Santa Claus, take pen to parchment, it brings me immense pleasure to introduce you to a tale spun by a remarkable adult who, much like the most spirited 8-year-olds, carries the flame of belief in the magic of Christmas.

In these pages, you will find not just a story, but a celebration of the enduring spirit that lights up the darkest winter nights. Decka's journey is a testament to the power of keeping the heart young, embracing the wonder that each holiday season brings. With every turn of the page, rediscover the timeless joy, kindness, and magic that make Christmas a season like no other.

So, dear readers, prepare yourselves to enter a realm where the imagination of an 8-year-old meets the insight of adulthood, and the magic of Christmas is not merely recalled but truly lived, cherished, and shared.

With festive cheer and a hearty 'Ho, Ho, Ho!',

Santa Claus

Prologue

It Just Is!

Illustration by A.M. & C.M.

Decka is a middle-aged man who continues to believe in the magic of Christmas. He just never stopped. If there's more than believing, then that's him. It's a natural instinct, kind of like breathing. The feeling of Christmas and everything that comes with it "Just Is."

There were a couple of times he almost forgot, but luckily, something or someone always reminded him. In fact, "Believe" isn't even the right word for him when it comes to Christmas. To Decka, believing isn't a choice; it's embedded in his soul.

Since as early as he can remember, the joy of Christmas has been intertwined with him, as naturally as his fingers and toes. The sound of jingling bells or Christmas music brings the biggest smile to his face. Even hearing someone say "Merry Christmas," whether directly to him or not, warms his heart just as much now as it did when he was a child, maybe even more. To Decka, a light display in a local park or the twinkling lights from a neighbor's window is more beautiful than any pricey excursion to a famous landmark.

Throughout the year, he could devour a bag of Oreos in one sitting, but they still wouldn't taste as good as a single Christmas cookie. There's something special to Decka about biting into a gingerbread man, perhaps because the little guy is smiling as he dips him into a glass of frosty white milk. And hot chocolate, whether with dancing marshmallows or a splash of bourbon, feels cozier to him than the warmest summer day. This is just a small glimpse of Decka's affection for Christmas.

Decka believes that right after Thanksgiving, everyone seems a little kinder and treats each other a little better. Sure, there are always a few Grinch's, but they seem to be the exception rather than the rule. He thinks everything improves during this time—like wearing pajamas. The fabric of regular pajamas and Christmas-themed ones might be identical, but for some reason, the red plaid ones feel like they just came out of a heavenly dryer every time he puts them on.

Decka may not be a psychiatrist, but he's noticed that people tend to forget about distant relatives for most of the year, only remembering them when wreaths start appearing on doors and it's time to send Christmas cards. These cards remind everyone that, no matter the time or distance, they are loved. Even the person you had a terrible fight with is game for mercy. In December, people realize that forgiveness is a strength and not a weakness. Decka knows that it's because of Christmas.

Amid the craziness and busyness of our lives, we often forget to let ourselves dream and embrace the unimaginable. The world remains full of unknowns, and anything is still possible if we allow ourselves to be open to it. You never know; if you reach high enough, your dreams might just come true.

You may think this is an untrue, make-believe story. Decka's story is a true, must-Believe story!

1
Waiting for Santa

Illustration by Melissa Dodson

Decka's real name is Derek, but he chooses to go by the nickname he gave himself inadvertently as a small child. Long story short, his parents tried to get him to pronounce his own name. He landed on Decka, and it stuck for a while. There were many years he went by his birth name but as you'll soon find out, he chose to revert to his preferred name. The one thing his parents gave him that he always appreciated was the best Christmases.

Too many decorations was not a phrase used in Decka's house. Wherever your eyes landed in any room, you were met with a glow of silver and gold or some kind of Christmas flare. Any available table was meant for maybe a snowman statue or bowl of candy canes. Every room needed to have garland somewhere. Whether it was a banister or just draping from the ceiling beams, you would be greeted with colors of white, silver, green, or red. Thankfully, OSHA never stopped over because there was so much Christmas clutter (or treasured relics) that you had to watch where you walked. The outside view was just as festive.

The porch was lit up so brightly that Decka would bet astronauts could see their house from space. Trees in the yard had as many ornaments and lights as the ones in the house. They had many lawn decorations, too. Everyone you can think of: a waving Santa, a Rudolph whose nose really lit red at night, a smiling snowman that stood next to Santa that also waved, and a bunch of Nutcracker-looking soldiers. They all lit up. Decka didn't even think about how high the electric bill was then, but his parents were never concerned, so neither was he.

Decka loved and still loves decorating. Back then, he would help his mom and dad as much as he could. If he couldn't reach a spot on the tree where he wanted to hang an ornament on, there was always someone there who was happy to lift him in the air to claim his spot. There was never criticism that the ornament was the "wrong color," "didn't look good there," "too many other ornaments were in that area," etc. Whatever he chose was perfect. Decka often laughs to himself when he hears adults struggling over the dressing up of a tree.

When it came to Christmas decorating (especially the tree), there was no wrong way. Just go for whatever the heart felt at the time. This is true for all ages. The only traditional thing that Decka loved (and still keeps) for decorating the tree is the very last part. Placing the angel on top of the tree. Decka's mom was kind of short, and the only time he would catch her on a ladder was once a year when the tree was ready for the grand finale.

The angel was made of gold porcelain with a sparkling finish. Her big white wings looked like they came from a heavenly butterfly. The face was very detailed and almost looked real. Blue eyes and a blissful smile gave her an extra peaceful aura. His mother always made sure the angel was securely placed on top of the tree, because if she fell, she could break, and it was one of her favorite Christmas decorations.

One of the many things that Decka loves about Christmas is the gathering of family and friends. Of the greatest presents he's been given in life, the one he loves the most is when he sees the excitement on familiar faces when people see each other during the festive season.

Whether it's someone who just saw their friend a day before or a relative who hasn't been seen since last Christmas, it's extra special when it's that cherished yuletide gathering. You know the one we're talking about. The party that happens once a year at someone's house or an annual reunion at a local tavern. Different members of your life celebrate in different ways, and many of you (like Decka) try to include everyone you can. As a youth, he would often have to go to three or four different houses through the weekends to attend all the different Christmas get-togethers. He loved it!

Nothing seemed more merry than the holiday hug he and everyone got when they walked through the door. Even the old musky smell from a grandparent or older aunt and uncle was somehow enjoyable. Nobody checked their watches and stayed until their eyes turned red, which meant it was time to drive home. The goodbyes were sad because the hellos were so happy.

Nothing has changed in middle-aged Decka's mind. He still celebrates with the same feelings he had as a little Decka. Sadly, some of the people have come and gone throughout the years, but he has never forgotten them.

Most years, Decka's mom and dad would open their house to everyone on Christmas Eve. Whether you were an immediate family member or some random stranger walking by, you would be welcome to walk into the house. The only stern warning you would be given is that you could be peer pressured to sing Christmas carols. That also would have depended on how many glasses of eggnog his grandmother had. The funniest thing about that was Decka's grandmother didn't drink except on Christmas Eve. It didn't take much before she was singing and convincing everyone else to join in. After all, how could anyone say no to grandma?

On this particular year, the party was going on as usual when Grandma and Grandpa declared it was getting late which meant two things. The first was that everyone should be careful getting home, being it was so late, and the other was so that Santa was coming. Decka needed to go to bed soon because the big man in red was on his way. He was having so much fun singing and playing with everyone that he almost forgot about Old Saint Nick.

As soon as everyone left, Decka hugged and kissed his parents' goodnight and then vaulted into bed. He pulled the covers over his head in hopes it would make him fall asleep faster. It was always tough for him to go to sleep on Christmas Eve. The youngster still had so much stimulation from everyone who had just left. On top of it, he was thinking about tomorrow. The big day!

Decka never gave much thought to presents under the tree. Well, except for the one year he wanted an Andre the Giant wrestling figure. Making a list for Santa was a struggle for him. Most years, he just picked things randomly out of a catalog to satisfy his mother. There was one year at the mall, the people waiting in line became increasingly impatient as Decka sat on Santa's lap and couldn't answer a simple question from the jolly one, "And what does Derek want for Christmas?" He was forced to use Decka's birth certificate name.

Truly not in need of anything, he replied, "Nothing, Santa, couldn't I just sit here and hang with you?"

Accompanied with a "Ho, Ho, Ho!" he replied, "I would love that. However, Christmas is a time of giving and being a good boy. I bet you want to give another child a chance to see Santa?"

"Just another couple minutes, Santa," Decka replied. "I bet I would make a good elf, Santa." he continued.

Santa was in a pickle, but luckily, Mom piped up, "Derek Santa is going to need to check on the elves."

Sadly, Decka understood and accepted the coloring book that Mrs. Claus offered as a parting gift.

Is this what Rudolph felt when the other reindeer wouldn't let him join their games? Decka thought, his heart sinking. He suddenly understood the red-nosed reindeer's loneliness, feeling just as excluded and unwanted.

Dragging and looking at his feet, he made his way straight down the candy lane walkway, which led to a fence door and out of Santa's life for another year. For just a few brief moments, Decka was heartbroken and felt rejected by Kris Kringle. He couldn't even look at him and just kept his head straight as he walked.

He didn't understand.

He didn't want a present and only wanted to be in Santa's company for a little while.

Before Decka made it all the way through the fence door, he heard a familiar voice. It was the man he was just talking to. It was Santa. "Merry Christmas Decka. We'll see you soon. Keep believing. Ho, Ho, Ho!"

Wait, he thought. *How did Old Saint Nick know my name is Decka? My mom made me use Derek.*

Decka turned around and strangely saw Santa already busy talking to another child who was climbing up on his lap. It didn't make any sense though, because it was almost like Santa was talking to him directly in his ear or maybe even from inside his head. Decka's mom was holding his hand the whole way down the candy cane lane and was curious why he stopped dead in his tracks.

"What's the matter, Honey?" she asked.

No answer came as he scanned his mind for any sign that he had misheard the voice. Nothing confirmed it, but Decka couldn't explain what just happened. He was confused and just looked at his mom and said, "Nothing, Mom."

"Decka, keep your eyes looking up at the stars on Christmas Eve." It was Santa's voice again. "Find the ones that twinkle like the lights on your Christmas tree. Ho! Ho! Ho!" Looking up at this mom, he could tell she didn't hear it. However, there was no mistaking it this time. He heard it loud and clear. Decka looked over at Santa a second time, and again the man in the red cap was laughing as the little girl sitting on his lap tugged on his beard. Close to pulling his hand away from his mother so he could go march right back up to Santa to confront him about his telepathy, the most incredible thing happened.

In the sea of statues within Santa's workshop were lit up penguins. They were dressed for the North Pole with white woolly hats and red scarves. The actual display was six of them set up in a circle as if they were ice skating in a small circle. Decka started to turn his head toward Santa's direction, and just about to whip his tiny hand out of his mother's, everything changed in his young life.

One of the penguins turned his own head towards Decka and slowly came to life. With a brightness in his eyes and a smile that formed out of nowhere, the penguin spoke, "Hey, Good Buddy! I know this is all brand new to you but take it from me. It's real! I'm real!" The penguin's voice was clear and reassuring.

"Just remember to look up at the sky on Christmas Eve. You won't miss it." The last thing he said before he returned to statue form was, "Oh yeah. Merry Christmas Decka!"

Before Decka could even process what had just happened, his mother tugged on his hand, only to be led out of the workshop and back into the rush of the mall shoppers. You'd think after what just happened, there was no way Decka's eyes were going to miss the Christmas Eve sky. How could he after what just occurred?

December 24th came and just as always, his house was full, and the celebration was in full effect. In the excitement of the festivities, Decka found himself eating all the delicious Christmas snacks like chocolate-covered pretzels, pumpkin cookies, various aged cheese and crackers, figs, roasted chestnuts, and tons and tons of hot chocolate. Needless to say, poor Decka got a little tummy ache that night. Eventually, he got an upset stomach and spent much of the night in the bathroom. His dad stayed with him in the bathroom for over an hour before declaring the worst part of the overindulgence had passed.

Coupled with the fact it was already late, Decka was completely exhausted. Sitting on the floor, poor Decka fell asleep right there and then. Wrapped in his father's arms, he was carried to his bed and was gently lowered into his bed. His dad kissed him on the forehead and whispered, "You'll be back to new by tomorrow, pal. Goodnight and Merry Christmas, son!"

At 8:35 the next morning, the first thing out of Decka's mouth wasn't "Did Santa come?" or "Merry Christmas, everybody!" It was, "Oh no, I missed it!"

He ran to the window and looked up at the sky just in case whatever he was supposed to see was still there. *Nothing.* The only thing up there were puffy white clouds and a bright blue sky that seemed to go on forever and ever.

Decka ran downstairs to see his parents sitting in the living room with their robes on and sipping coffee. They smiled, and both declared in sync, "Santa came!"

Even the dog Sparkles was wagging his tail and seemed to speak. Both smiling and still talking at the same time, "He brought you lots of presents. He knew you were a good boy this year."

Of course, he already knew Santa thought that. He just didn't know what he was supposed to see in the sky the night before. He missed his chance.

For the next few years on Christmas Eve, Decka would stare up at the stars and wonder what he was supposed to see that night. The mystery never left him as he even found himself glancing up during random times in the year to hopefully see what he was supposed to see.

Maybe one day, he would find out.

2
The Most Sadful-est Time of the Year

AI image by Bill Mayer

Decka was disappointed that he missed seeing whatever he was supposed to see but didn't dwell on it for too long. His young mind was easily distracted by gifts under the Christmas tree. Present after present was opened in a frenzy. Each one torn open was better than the one he had just ripped open before.

"I can't believe this is for me! This is the best gift ever!" he would declare. Decka never really cared what he got. He was just happy with the surprise in the box. A pair of socks was just as exciting as a new toy robot.

A special pancake breakfast with whip cream that resembled Santa's face briefly reminded Decka of the "night light" display he missed. He was enjoying his day so much that he shrugged it off as bad timing and convinced himself, *if it's meant to be, he'll get a second chance one day.* As he was thinking, his dad did a messy hair rub, and he gleefully chomped away at the sugary Santa pancake.

"Hurry up, buddy. We need to leave in about an hour to go to Uncle Pete's." Pete was his father's brother who opened his house to immediate, extended, friends, friends of friends, and anyone who wanted to come to his joyous gathering. Frankly, it meant more Christmas celebrating and the better for Decka. He doubled the pancake munching so he wouldn't miss the caravan about to leave.

Decka waited outside with his dad while the car was packed with more presents. As his dad strategically arranged the packages in the trunk like a perfect Tetris puzzle, Decka gazed over at the front lawn and all the displays out there and thought again about the talking penguin. It was real. At least that day it was. Decka walked over to the front lawn and started poking at them.

First, Rudolph. "Hey, anybody in there?"

No response from the plastic animal.

Next was the snowman. "Hello?"

Again, just an object made up of a man-made substance.

Santa and the nutcracker soldiers all got the same treatment with the same response.

Maybe it's only the penguins that are alive, Decka pondered.

Beep, Beep.

His mom and dad were waving for Decka to get in the car that had finally been loaded. "Time to go!" Dad announced through the rolled-down window.

The mystery was ongoing. It was winter, so safe to say it was a cold case yet to be solved.

The next days after Christmas were busy, but not as hectic. He didn't have school, so Decka spent most of the days playing with his neighborhood friends. They all compared presents and bragged about what Santa had brought them all. Even though it was technically after December 25th, these were part of the festivities according to Decka. As great and perfect as everything was for the last month or so, something was about to happen that brought all the fun to a screeching halt.

It was getting late, so Decka knew it wouldn't be long before his mother yelled for him to come home. He said goodbye to his friends and walked down the sidewalk to his home. He drew in a deep breath, savoring the aroma of chimneys exhaling wisps of fireplace scents along his street. The scent of burning oak and cedar was the finest fragrance he had ever smelled. Just another millionth reason that he loved Christmas.

Decka walked through the front door, flicked both his left and right glove off at the same time and asked what was for dinner. "The leftover ham and vegetables are just about ready, so don't go too far." she answered.

There was so much food at Uncle Pete's that they were forced to take some with them when they left. Nobody minded the second helping, and his mom was considerate enough to give it a few days between, so at least it wasn't back-to-back the same menu.

Smelling the food, it didn't seem worth it to play with a toy or start a Christmas movie, so Decka parked himself at the dinner table. That's when the worst words of words came out of his mom's mouth, "Derek, we're going to take the decorations down tomorrow. Can you help me, and Dad take 'em down?"

His heart stopped, and suddenly wasn't hungry anymore. As happy as the Christmas season made Decka, the opposite was true when it was time it ended. It would take days and days to put up all the Christmas decorations, but somehow only one to take them all down. When his mother felt it was time, there was no stopping it. She went from hot to cold in a millisecond. For Decka, it was a long and slow march toward gloom. He didn't understand why it all had to end. He even tried begging a couple times.

"Mom, can't we just leave it up?" he asked.

"Sorry, need the space," her face was expressionless.

Space for what? Decka thought. He knew it was just an excuse.

"How about just another month, Ma?"

"No, it's happening tomorrow," she said, putting her foot down. "Starting early in the morning."

There was no getting out of it. Christmas was over for another year.

After dinner, Decka sat on the living room floor and stared at the tree all night. He tried to take in as much as he could of the light and somehow soak in the feeling to make it last until next year. He needed to preserve every remaining moment before it all got stored away in the attic. Eventually, his parents told him it was time to go to bed. Once again, he asked for a delay in things, but just like his request to not take the decorations down, he was denied. He eventually managed to pick himself off the floor and slowly climbed the stairs to his bedroom. One last glance before he would see the tree and everything illuminated with lights.

Decka sighed and quietly spoke, "Goodbye Christmas."

He crawled into bed, pulled the blanket over his head, and let his tears rain into the pillow.

The next morning came and by the time Decka made it downstairs, his mother and father had already packed away things. The dining room and hallways were almost already garland-free. He quickly looked out the front window and was happy that at least the lawn displays were still up. He knew they would be coming down within hours, but at least he got to see them one more time.

"What do you want for breakfast?" Mom asked.

"I'm not really hungry. I can start helping," Decka replied.

"Are you sure?" she asked a second time.

"Yes, Mom!" Decka answered in a convincing manner.

"Okay, you can start taking the ornaments off the tree," she continued. "Just be careful packing them away so they don't break."

Decka was a little hungry, but he didn't want to miss any of the good ornaments being put away. If he was being forced to put Christmas out of its apparent misery, he thought he should at least be the one to do it. He hesitantly started packing away. Slowly he would grab an ornament off the tree, carefully wrap it in bubble wrap, and place it in its designated storage bin. The first ones he would grab would be his favorites. Amongst these were Superman, a yellow lab with a Santa hat, and a polar bear with skis. With each reluctant takedown of an ornament, Decka would glare as almost to give them their own farewell. To him, they wouldn't be seen again for almost another year.

A few hours passed, and almost all the decorations were packed in crates and boxes. His father started bringing them upstairs building piles close to the attic door. Decka continued to help downstairs. He noticed that his mother packed the angel on top of the tree extra carefully. He just couldn't understand if something was so important to someone, why they would pack it away for a year.

Wouldn't you enjoy it all the time? he thought.

Eventually, everything was taken down including the fake tree, which was also ushered up the stairs in what seemed like an extra struggle for his father. Immediately, his mother started vacuuming where some pine needles had fallen. There was a lot more light shining through the window where the tree had been, which most people would have welcomed. But not Decka. He would have been happy seeing the big, 'ole beautiful Christmas tree blocking the outside.

He eventually went upstairs to get out of the path and annoying loudness of the vacuum. His father was just coming down the attic stairs from his wrestling match with the tree. It was a tough fight, but it looked like his dad had won. Decka was small, but his father thought he could still be useful.

"Decka, that pile over there is very light." Pointing with his finger. "If you think they're light enough, grab one and bring them up. Be careful going up and down the stairs."

He had never been up to the attic before, so he was intrigued by the new responsibility that had been bestowed upon him. Decka grabbed a box and walked up the wooden staircase that curled to the left. His eyes were met with a gigantic sea of wood that made up the walls, floor, and ceiling. It seemed so empty and brown. He heard his dad's feet coming up behind him as he was stopped at the top step.

"Keep going bud. All the way to the back," his father instructed. Decka looked further down the attic and located a Christmas tree branch peeking from under a blanket all the way down the end of the attic. His dad must have laid that over the tree to protect it somehow.

Starting to make his way down to the end of the attic, he noticed there was lots of dust and that had to be the reason it was covered up. It made sense to keep it protected. However, Decka also didn't appreciate how just a few hours ago the tree was the center place of the living room glowing with majestic lights. A great display for not just his family; but proudly for the whole neighborhood to see. Now, it was thrown on the floor so carelessly. His father shuffled past where Decka was still standing and processing what he was seeing. His dad plopped a box on top of another box very carelessly. *How could he be so hasty?* All the items in those boxes brought so much joy and happiness for the last month or so.

"Keep going Derek," his dad urged him. He must have noticed the thoughts and stalling that was going on in Decka's mind. With his small legs and muscles, Decka continued moving back and forth. There weren't many boxes that were light enough for Decka to move compared to the volume his dad had, but it didn't matter in the amount of what was getting accomplished. His dad moved three boxes to his one without breaking a sweat.

Still, with every trip, Decka became more and more depressed. He started to notice more details about the attic with every journey he made. It wasn't very bright in there with only a few light bulbs to light it up. It was also cold and considering the small sweat he started working up, meant it was even colder than he was experiencing. Maybe that's what the blanket over the tree was really for, to keep the tree warm, not from collecting dust.

Eventually, Decka ran out of boxes and could only watch his father bring the remaining up. He could have waited out in the hallway, but instead found a random crate to sit on so he could supervise his father's work. It wasn't much longer before he noticed his dad started bringing up the lawn decorations. Rudolph, Santa, soldiers, etc. He sarcastically laughed to himself, "Maybe the snowman will like the cold up there."

A few more random items and his father stopped at the end, turned around, clapped, rubbed his palms together, and in an almost celebratory declaration, said, "Well, that's it for another year!"

He walked back toward the staircase and said, "Come on, buddy." Decka stood up from the box he was on and turned back to look at all the Christmas spirit stuffed into boxes and jammed into the far end of an attic to be forgotten about for another year. He went down two steps but could still see everything at the end of the attic by just looking over the top stair. His dad turned off the light switch that was located on a beam near the stairs.

It was pitch black in there now and looked more dreadful and discarded. The light that came from the hallway below was the only reason you could make out where the stairs were.

Decka looked back one last time and, with a heavy heart and using the words his dad just did, whispered to himself, "Well, that's it for another year."

3
July 4th

Illustration by Darryl Greenlee

Next to Christmas, the Fourth of July was one of Decka's favorite holidays. There were a lot of friends and families around, plenty of food, people laughing, music playing, etc. Instead of scenes of silver and gold seen throughout the neighborhoods, a person could marvel at decorations with red, white, and blue. Rather than the smell of logs in fireplaces, the odor of hot dogs and hamburgers could be smelled from yards and yards away. The sounds of jingle bells ringing throughout the neighborhoods were now children laughing with every cannonball plunge into a pool somewhere.

As he grew older, he discovered an additional adult reason to cherish both Christmas and Independence Day: they were among the few occasions when the mail person didn't deliver bills that he would struggle to pay.

Decka was twenty-five when this particular summer's extravaganza would be held at his neighbor's house. He was excited and looked forward to seeing old and new friends for the annual celebration. Although he wasn't the host, he felt it was just as important to help as much as possible so it would be the most fun as could be. The night before, he even assisted his neighbor Jerry with setting up tables, cleaning off lawn seats that had been stored in the shed since the previous Independence Day.

When all was done and ready to go, Jerry said, 'Well, D-Man, might as well start now.' He ran into the house, grabbed a couple bottles of beer, and handed one to Decka. Twisting the cap off, Decka sat down on top of the cooler that would be full of more beer and ice tomorrow.

"Thanks, Jerry, and thanks again for hosting."

"Looks like it's going to be a good day weather-wise," Jerry replied as he reached out for a toast.

Clinking his bottle in response, Decka continued, "It's supposed to be for sure. I'll finish making macaroni and potato salad tonight, then grab more beer and ice in the morning. Anything else we need that I can't think of?"

"I think we've got it all covered, bro," Jerry replied, tapping his tablet to adjust the volume of the music streaming through the outdoor speakers. Decka recognized the lively tunes as a playlist only Jerry could curate, a testament to his tech-savvy nature. As Decka assisted with the preparations, he couldn't help but notice the array of gadgets scattered around. A tablet effortlessly controlled the music, while a sleek portable speaker emitted crystal-clear sound. It was evident that Jerry cherished his gadgets as much as he did hosting gatherings.

Beyond the outdoor speakers and music-controlling tablets, Decka recalled visiting Jerry's house on other occasions and being greeted by the latest TVs and computers. It seemed Jerry consistently stayed ahead in the tech game, always upgrading his arsenal to ensure the best experience for himself and his guests. It was another reflection of Jerry's passion for electronics and his commitment to crafting the ultimate entertainment environment.

Decka finished his beer and went home to prepare his dishes for the next day.

Around 10:00 the next morning, Decka ran to the beer store and bought a couple thirty-packs and about six bags of ice. He dropped half of the beers and half of the ice in Jerry's cooler. There wasn't enough room for all, and he wanted to keep half of it cool, so he brought it home and put it in his own fridge and freezer for safe storage. When they needed to refill, he would just run home and grab the backup. This was a once-a-year gathering, so even if there were leftovers, it was par for the course.

Decka went over to Jerry's about an hour later, and amazingly, a couple people had already arrived. The weather and event were perfect this year, so he could tell it was going to be a fun and full-packed cookout. One of the people already there was Jerry's brother Carmine, but the other was unfamiliar to Decka. She was beautiful, and he would have definitely remembered her previously. Being the perfect host, Jerry quickly provided an introduction.

"Derek, this is Alicia," introducing her with a nod toward the newcomer.

"She's our new neighbor down the street, just moved in about a month ago." Shaking her hand, Decka replied, "Hi, nice to meet you. I assume yours is the red house a few houses down?"

"Yes, that's me." Alicia smiled and asked, "Where do you live?"

"Oh, I live even farther and have a long drive home tonight," he replied with a playful grin. "Actually, I live right there," pointing over the fence to his house.

"Oh, okay." She chuckled back and looked back at Jerry. "What can I help with?"

"I'm about all set here, Alicia," Jerry answered. "There are beers in the cooler or drink whatever you want and just enjoy yourself."

She said thanks and grabbed a beer she must have brought herself out of the cooler and found a lawn chair to sit in. Making sure she was far enough away, Jerry whispered in Decka's ear, "Hey, D-Man, what do you think of her?"

Decka responded just as discreetly, "Obviously gorgeous. How come I didn't notice she moved in?"

"Not sure why the house never had a sale sign on it, but I saw her walking by the other day, and she told me she had just moved in," he continued. "She seemed nice, and so I invited her."

"I also figured you're single, and maybe she is too," Jerry finished.

"You're funny, man, but who knows? Maybe she's psycho," Decka replied, grabbed a beer himself, and went to catch up with Carmine.

A few hours later, cars for Jerry's and other neighbor's cookouts filled the street. Jerry was always a great host. He was older but somehow never missed a beat and was able to balance grilling, bartending, and socializing. Decka would occasionally step in and help flip a burger or two, but for the most part, Jerry would run the show. The music was blasting, people were chatting it up, and everyone seemed to be having a great time being together.

Well, everyone except the other neighbors Decka was about to meet. Many for the first time, some for the second time in a very long time.

The beer and ice in the cooler at Jerry's were starting to get a little low, so Decka decided to go grab the backup stored in his house. "Going to grab some refills, Jerry," he announced.

"Okay, D-Man!" Jerry replied.

On his walk over to his house, Alicia asked, "Need any help, Derek?"

"Thanks, I should be all set," he replied. He noticed for the second time how nice she seemed.

Decka walked over and into his kitchen from the side door that he had left unlocked. Making a quick left to the fridge, he grabbed the other thirty-pack and opened the freezer to grab another bag of ice. He closed the freezer door and was about to make an about-face and go right back out of the house when he heard something strange.

It sounded like music. Music coming from the attic. He put the beer and ice on the counter as if somehow it would make his hearing better. He listened closer. For sure, it was music. Coming from above. He started to make out the lyrics of the song being sung.

A song he remembered from his childhood. It was the words to "Cruel Summer" sung by an eighties trio called Bananarama. Decka was sure it wasn't their version, though. For starters, they were a girl band and second, whoever was singing it was doing it acapella.

He thought harder. Did he have an old radio up there that somehow came on by itself? Then he realized the only thing he had up there were Christmas decorations and a humidifier that he put up there to keep all the decorations safe from moisture. The only other option was there were burglars in the house. This didn't make any sense, though. His attic was fairly small and there was no way in or out from the outside. Why would a burglar, or a few of them, hide themselves in the attic? He did leave his door open and it could be possible that they saw him coming and scooted up there. Either way, Decka needed to confront the sound.

Decka grabbed a baseball bat that leaned against the fireplace and made his way to the attic entrance. Unlike his parents' house, he didn't have stairs but rather a pulldown ladder. This also made it stranger that people would be up there and singing eighties tunes. Either way, he pulled down the stairs with his left hand while holding the bat in his right. Prepared to pounce on the first thing he saw, he slowly pulled the ladder down and even slower creaked up the ladder.

He thrust his head upward, shouting with force, "WHAT ARE YOU DOING IN MY HOUSE!?"

In an instant, Decka dropped his bat and nearly tumbled off the ladder. Simultaneously, a plastic snowman, two light-up reindeer, and lawn penguin came to an abrupt stop, frozen in their tracks at the line of "Leaving Me Here on My Own."

All present parties stood motionless and silent in perfect synchrony.

Emerging from his daze, Decka surveyed the scene. He noticed they were all sitting on boxes covered in gift wrap. As his focus sharpened, Decka's gaze roamed the walls, taking in his Christmas decorations spread throughout the space. They were displayed in a way probably better than he could do himself. The Christmas lights swayed from beam to beam, and garlands hugged the walls. Decka also noticed the white stuffing on the floor, creating the illusion of snow-covered ground. A smile warmed his cheeks as he observed the Polar Express train chugging along the tracks, encircling models of a beautifully lit-up Christmas town.

He was in a trance again, but this time he wasn't shocked at what he saw, but rather amazed.

"Um, Decka?"

As he snapped back to reality, he found himself face to face with the characters he had just witnessed singing. "Decka? How do you know that name, and I'm sorry, what is happening here?" he asked, clearly confused.

"Well, Decka, we all know you," chimed in the penguin, his words slightly stuttered by the shape of his narrow beak. "I actually had a conversation with you back when you were a younger Decka at the mall," he continued, the slight lisp adding an endearing quality to his voice. "I may have looked a little different back then, but I'm still the same on the inside. Good Buddy."

"Good Buddy? Wait, I remember that!" Decka exclaimed.

The penguin elaborated, "I've... I mean, a few of us have been around this whole time."

"We even remember when you tried to communicate with us on your front lawn that Christmas morning," added one of the reindeer, whose voice had a distinctly feminine tone that was calm and assuring.

"Can you all talk?" Decka inquired.

"We sure can, Decka," replied the other reindeer, now speaking in a deep voice that resonated with bass, perfectly matching his antlers.

Suddenly, a knock echoed at the door, accompanied by Jerry's voice. "Derek, where are the cold ones, man?"

Realization struck me like a bolt of lightning. It had been several minutes, and I hadn't brought the beer and ice over to Jerry's, despite being mere feet and a fence away.

"Hold on one sec, I'll be right back," Decka let everyone know.

He never ended up making it all the way up the ladder with all this new wonderment, so it was a lot quicker to go back down. He rapidly climbed down, closed the opening to the attic, and darted to the kitchen door where Jerry was waiting.

"Hey, D-Man, I thought you got lost," Jerry said, peering through the screen door with a teasing grin.

Not being able to explain what he just saw to himself yet, Decka was not going to tell his neighbor what he just witnessed. He knew he needed to get back up to the attic ASAP. He started to think of a reason to excuse himself from the Fourth of July Party. Luckily, Jerry provided just the excuse he needed.

"Hey, are you alright? Jerry asked. "You look a little out of it right now."

This was just the break Decka needed. Apparently, the first meeting of talking Christmas decorations in the attic showed on his face.

"Um, actually, Jerry," he said, displaying his best acting skills, "I don't feel so great right now," his voice wavering slightly to sell the performance. He walked over to the beer and ice that were still on the kitchen counter. "Here ya go. I think I have a stomach bug or something."

Continuing, he added, "I'm sorry, but I might have to lay down for a little bit,"

"Man, sorry to hear that," Jerry replied. "Won't be the same without ya."

"If you feel better later, you know we'll be out there all night." He finished and walked back to his yard with the beer and ice.

Decka closed the door and locked it this time. He also went to the living room where he closed and locked that door as well. He couldn't have any interruptions. There were so many questions about to be asked.

4
Leaving Me Here on My Own

Illustration by Jackson Register

Decka made his way back to the attic. This time, his pace was the opposite of thinking there was a burglar up there. He calmly made his way up the stairs and slowly pushed open the door. For a split second, he thought maybe it would go back to the boring old attic with everything safely packed in boxes. However, he knew he saw what he saw ... and heard for that matter.

He made his way all the way up this time, and everybody was still there but this time they were quietly waiting. They weren't caught red-handed belting out a song and, in fact, seemed to be waiting for him.

Decka looked around for somewhere to sit. As his eyes were surveilling the room, he felt a milk cart being pushed behind his calves. He looked back and the female reindeer nudged it with her nose, as an offering of a seat to sit on.

"Thank you," Decka said, while lowering himself to sit, his mind still trying to process the surreal.

The female reindeer went back to the others who were already sitting themselves. Everyone was sitting as if this was a campfire. The milk crate Decka was sitting on was a perfect height to see everyone close-up and eye to eye. His shock was over. He then laughed to himself and spoke first.

"Okay, this is crazy, but it also doesn't seem to be for some reason," Decka said with a bemused smile, his eyes shifting between each of the fantastical creatures surrounding him.

The penguin spoke up, breaking the silence, "I'm sure you have a lot of questions."

"We'll do our best to explain them," he continued, his voice calm and reassuring.

Decka nodded, feeling overwhelmed by the situation. "I don't even know what to ask first," he admitted.

But then, a question formed in his mind. "Well, how about...How?" he asked, voicing his confusion.

The penguin, reindeer, and snowman exchanged glances, silently communicating before the penguin spoke again, "Spirit."

"We all have spirit," he stated matter-of-factly, his tone carrying a hint of wisdom.

Decka's confusion only deepened. "Like the spirit of a ghost?" he ventured.

"No, no, not that kind of spirit," the penguin clarified, offering further explanation. "Everyone has spirit. It's like a way of being and going about things. What makes them tick. For example, if you're feeling mopey, you act mopey. That's having a mopey spirit."

"Yeah, exactly," chimed in the male reindeer. "Some people are happy all the time and have happy spirits."

"There are all kinds of different spirits, too," the snowman chimed in joyfully, his voice carrying a childlike wonder and innocent glee that seemed to embody the pure happiness of freshly fallen snow.

"Right, and some people even have multiple spirits," added the female reindeer.

The penguin resumed the conversation, his voice reassuring as he addressed Decka directly. "You have an additional spirit that not many have," he explained, his gaze locked onto Decka's, searching for understanding.

"At least not a lot of people have a lot of anymore," he added with a hint of sadness, his eyes drifting upwards as if contemplating something beyond the attic roof.

Then, he turned back to Decka, a warm smile gracing his features. 'You have real Christmas spirit,' he remarked, his tone tinged with hopefulness.

The snowman eagerly jumped in, adding, "And one of the most and biggest Christmas spirits of all!"

He was still trying to wrap his head around everything, knowing he'd need more clarification later.

"Can all of you talk?" Decka asked, directing his question to anyone who might answer.

The penguin nodded.

Decka's curiosity sparked another question. "So, are you the leader?" he inquired.

The penguin burst into even more laughter. "Hahahahaha, nope," he replied between chuckles. "We don't have a leader. Well, except for Santa, I guess."

Decka hurriedly tried to clarify his question, realizing another one was surfacing. "I didn't mean, like, are you alien-like beings who answer to a leader?"

"Wait, did you just say Santa?" Decka's eyes widened with excitement. "Do you talk to him?"

The snowman chimed in, "See, that's what I'm talking about when I say biggest Christmas spirits of all. You don't even question if Santa is real."

"Well, of course he's real," Decka declared confidently. "He just is! He talked to me at the mall when I was eight."

Reflecting, he gazed at the attic ceiling, memories flooding back in an instant. "He gave me a chance to see something on Christmas Eve, and I didn't" he confessed. "I went to see him year after year, hoping for another chance. I wanted to ask him so many times, but I was always a little ashamed."

A heavy silence settled over the room as Decka's Christmas companions absorbed his words.

"Hey, Good Buddy," the penguin waddled over and draped his wing around Decka's shoulder. "Santa saw what happened that night. He knows you were sick from eating all those Christmas goodies."

"Really?" Decka asked, surprised by the revelation.

The penguin nodded reassuringly. "He knows everything. He even knows how you whispered to him in the mall every year."

"He heard that?" Decka's eyes widened in amazement.

"He heard you every time," the male reindeer confirmed. "Even last year."

Overwhelmed, Decka whispered, "I can't believe it. I just hoped he might catch me going by and give me a second chance."

"I know you want to know what was in the sky, but someday, I'm sure Santa will tell you himself," the female reindeer comforted, joining the penguin in comforting Decka.

Things were just starting to make sense – well, a little bit, anyway. There were still so many questions he had.

"So why am I just seeing you now?"

This was a major question that formed in his mind over the time he'd been getting to know his new friends in the attic.

"Who wants to take this one?" the penguin asked. "Oh, I guess I will," he answered his own question.

The penguin then explained, "Well, honestly, we were thinking about waiting another few years until you hit about thirty before we revealed ourselves. However, you caught us singing."

"Yeah, I am going to get to why you were singing that song in a sec," Decka said while almost laughing at the same time. He felt a little better about Santa not being disappointed in him. "But why thirty?"

"We obviously hear everything down there and didn't want to add any more stress on your life."

"Like what kind of stress?" Decka asked.

"Well, you have a full time job that doesn't pay enough of the bills. You're barely keeping the roof over your head." He kept going, "It's not because you don't work enough. You put in more than enough hours and even try to get overtime when you can. But it's still not enough."

Decka was surprised they knew all these personal details.

"You couldn't even really afford to buy that beer and ice today, but you did, and we know why you did."

Decka raised his finger to answer, but before he could answer was interrupted.

"You did it because you didn't want to miss the Fourth of July with Jerry and everyone."

Decka's face twisted in bewilderment. "Okay, yes, I have money problems, but what does that have to do with you guys and me being able to see you?"

The male reindeer joined in. "This might seem like a silly excuse, but we thought if you finally knew we were around, you would concentrate on us and Christmas, which you do all year anyway."

He explained further, "If you spent more time thinking about Christmas than you already do, you would stop thinking about yourself and what you need."

The female reindeer walked away from Decka's side and joined the male reindeer's side. It seemed clear to Decka that somehow, they were best friends themselves. Like in a soulmate type of way. She continued what he was trying to say, "And because you know Christmas is about Giving, you wouldn't think about anything else and might make yourself more broke than maybe you already are."

"I think I get it...kind of," Decka said.

"We didn't want to be the cause of you losing anything." the penguin summed everything up in one statement. "Including the house."

This brought up more questions.

"Wait! If this house goes away, will you guys go away?" Decka concerningly asked.

The snowman took this one. "Not at all. We're all here in spirit and in specific Christmas spirit, and as long as we have spirit, we can be anywhere at anytime and in any place."

He wasn't done. "Ya see, Decka, the reason we can all see each other is because we have always loved Christmas, and we know what Christmas is about. It's about Giving. We would be selfish about revealing ourselves, knowing you might give more of your time to us. We couldn't do that."

He finalized his thought with, "We always knew we'd be together one day anyways, so we just figured we'd wait until things settled down for you."

Decka was appreciative. He had learned so much in a short amount of time, but there were still so many questions to be answered. He needed to process everything he had learned to this point. However, there was still one question he was curious about. It wasn't the most important question, but for some reason he needed to know sooner rather than later.

"Can I ask one more question for now?"

"I'm sure you have many more, Good Buddy, but go for it." the penguin responded.

"Why on Earth were you all singing Cruel Summer by Bananarama?" Decka asked in a humorous manner.

This seemed like the simplest question so far, yet it was anything but.

"Once in a while, we get lonely up here all by ourselves." The male reindeer said.

"Now, don't get us wrong. We love it up here. You have it temperature-controlled and treat us better than anyone. But sometimes we miss being out and displayed for everyone to see." He did his best to explain further. "As soon as Christmastime is over, most people just put their decorations away somewhere and forget about it for eleven months. As fast as people put us out and displayed, we are forgotten about just as quickly. How can we bring so much joy to people's lives and, in the same instance, be discarded just as easily."

"As far as the Fourth of July and summertime fun, we know Christmas is the furthest thing from everyone's mind."

The female reindeer finished with, "For us, it's always a Cruel Summer, and we're left on our own."

Decka felt terrible, and it showed on his face.

The penguin who had been sitting stood up. "Okay, enough of this sad stuff."

"No, I get it," Decka responded to her story. He tried to defend himself, "I can't even tell you how many times I tried to throw a Christmas in July party, but nobody would come."

The female reindeer "Oh, I didn't mean you. We all know you're with us. I was talking about in general and the whole wide world.

"Just basically, we have to entertain ourselves when we feel forgotten about." the penguin said. "It's no big deal."

"Well, I'll never think of that song the same way again," Decka offered. He felt it was time to turn the conversation back to a happy one.

"Hey, wait here one sec." He jumped up from the milk crate and made his way down the ladder to the main level of the house. He yelled up to the attic as he glided through the house. His newly found house roommates wondered what he was doing.

"Two minutes!" he yelled up.

In less than one minute, Decka came back up through the attic dressed in his Christmas pajamas.

"There, this is better!" he declared and plopped back down on the milk crate.

"Okay, I still have soooooooooo many questions, but my brain is pretty worn out. How about we all sing a few songs on this Fourth of July?"

The penguin, snowman, and reindeers looked at each other and smiled from as wide as could be.

"Okay, do we sing Cruel Summer?" Decka asked. "I know most of the words, and either way can look up the lyrics on my phone. Or we just sing Christmas songs."

"How about both?" the male reindeer.

"Yeah!" everyone said at the same time.

There was still a Fourth of July party going on next door. However, a few yards away a separate party was going on. It started with a bitter-sweet summer song, followed by joyous Christmas carols.

It wasn't until they were into their fifth or sixth Christmas song that Decka thought about something that the female reindeer said. She mentioned something about the "Whole Wide World." How would he know that the whole wide world forgot about them? After they finished singing the song they were on, Decka raised his hand to indicate he had a question.

"Sorry, I promise this is the last question for the night," he said, seeking confirmation. "Are there more of you all over the world?"

They all laughed. "Not only are there more of us all over the world, but there are also more of us here in this attic."

Now only the penguin spoke, "Every decoration up here is full of life and Christmas spirit. They don't like our singing of 'Cruel Summer,' so they've been napping all day." He continued, "You'll probably meet the rest of them tomorrow."

Decka couldn't believe everything that had happened that day could get any better, but it was about to. They all started singing a new song. It happened to be his favorite song: "Happy Holidays" probably best known sung by Andy Williams. A few more songs later he started getting sleepy. He was comfortable and decided to just lay on the attic floor and fall asleep there.

It was summer, and yet he was going to sleep with a dream of red cardinals chirping around snow-filled pine trees lit up by twinkling North Pole stars.

The male and female reindeer whispered to each other to not wake their new friend.

"That was a lot," said the female.

"Sure was," responded the male "We didn't get to even tell him the most magical thing of all yet."

Together, they found an old blanket and used their hoofs to cover sleeping Decka.

"Goodnight, Good Buddy!"

5
Believing

Illustration by Laura Kaye

Decka's blurry eyes slowly opened the next morning. Everything seemed a little cloudy, and at first, he wasn't sure where he was. As things came into focus, he noticed the string of sparkling lights swaying from the rafters. He thought to himself that somehow a breeze must get into the attic to make them sway from side to side. The first thing he heard was the train going around on the track. He couldn't see it chugging along just yet, but it was too familiar a sound to be anything else. He could smell the pine from the Christmas tree. If he didn't know any better, he was waking up on Christmas morning.

"Good morning, Good Buddy!" Decka lifted his head and saw the penguin sitting close watching over him.

"Good morning...um." Decka started to shake off his morning daze. "I just realized I don't know what your name or anyone's name is."

"Well, what do you want our names to be? You can call us whatever you want," the penguin replied.

"How about just Penguin, Snowman, and, well...I need to come up with different names other than 'Reindeer' since there are two," Decka suggested.

"That's perfect," the penguin responded, delving into the discussion further. "Here, we get to be what we want to be and be called whatever we choose. We basically pick our own names."

Decka considered this and said, "Forget what I said a few minutes ago. I'll call you by your chosen names."

"I actually have always liked penguins, so I'm a Christmas penguin. I like the name, Bill, too, because it goes with my bill here," the penguin gestured towards his orange mouth area. "But for you to call me Penguin is perfect because that's what I am. By the way, can I ask you a question, Decka?"

"Sure."

"Why do you let people call you Derek when you prefer Decka?" the penguin inquired.

"Well, it's what my parents named me, so it was just the grown-up thing to do," Decka explained.

"Yeah, but Decka is the name you chose," the penguin challenged.

"I guess you're right," he pondered. "Honestly, I don't mind being called Derek, and I'm used to it, but Decka was what I would have chosen for myself."

"Well, then you should go by what you feel is you, and it sounds like Decka is who you feel you are," the penguin encouraged.

"You're so right! From now on, I'm going to ask people to call me Decka," he declared. "I won't get mad if they don't, but my preferred name is Decka, and I shouldn't feel bad about it."

"Now you're talking, Decka!" the penguin cheered.

"Thanks for the pep talk, Bill!" Decka purposely used the name he chose for himself.

"Now, there's something we need to tell you that you might want to be sitting down for," Bill the Penguin said.

"Oh no, what is it?" Decka asked.

"It's nothing bad at all," Bill reassured him. "In fact, it's quite wonderful, just a little hard to explain."

Just as the night before, the female reindeer pushed the milk carton under him to sit. "My name is Dear," she said.

"And I'm Rayne," said the other male deer.

Decka loved the play on their names and sat on the milk carton. "Okay, what's the something you need to tell me?"

Bill the Penguin started to explain, "Weeeell."

DING DONG! Everyone's head turned towards the attic doorway in unison. Someone was ringing the doorbell. For a moment, Decka thought about ignoring it but thought he better see who it was.

"Hold that thought!" he told the others. "Let me see who's at the door. It's probably just Jerry."

Decka scurried down the attic ladder and made his way to the front door. He opened the door expecting Jerry, but was surprised at who was there. It was Alicia.

"Hi, I hope I'm not bothering you. Jerry told me you weren't feeling good last night, and I wanted to see if you are feeling better and if you need anything."

Decka was immediately conflicted with emotions. He thought it was the sweetest thing for Alicia whom he just met, to check on him, but he felt terrible for lying about being sick. He was also going to have to lie again to cover his actions. It's not like he could just tell her that while they were enjoying Fourth of July fireworks, he was belting out "Deck the Halls" with living Christmas Decorations. On top of it, he didn't even understand everything yet and how could he even begin to explain.

"You are definitely not bothering me at all." He noticed she was even more beautiful today which was going to make it even harder to fib. "I feel a lot better, thanks." he continued. "I think I just had something that didn't agree with me."

He wanted to say more, but he just stood there frozen. For a moment, he wanted to ask her out but didn't think he had a shot, so he just said nothing.

"Well if you need anything, you know where I live." She smiled, turned, walked down the three brick stairs, and started down the walkway.

"Wait!" Decka shouted.

Alicia turned around and waited for whatever was so urgent to be said.

Again, he froze and couldn't get out what he wanted to, which was to ask her out on a date.

"Um, I just wanted to thank you again," he said, almost in an embarrassing way. "It was really cool of you to check on me. I appreciate it."

She smiled again. "No problem. Hey, at least the fourth was a Saturday this year, and we have an extra day to recover."

"Yeah, I definitely appreciate that," he replied. He wished her a goodbye and closed the front door. He then realized what an idiot he probably sounded like.

He returned to the attic to continue the big conversation that was (in his mind) pleasantly interrupted.

Ready for the conversation that was supposed to begin, he was slightly caught off guard when another one came up.

"Why didn't you ask her out?" Rayne the Reindeer asked.

"Yeah, Good Buddy, how come you didn't ask her on a date?" Bill asked.

"I think she likes you," Rayne reiterated.

Decka looked at the snowman for his contribution, who just looked at the others and said, "What they said."

"I haven't caught your name yet," he responded to the snowman.

"My name is Scarf, and I definitely think you should ask Alicia out."

"Decka laughed out loud and asked if they could always hear his conversations in the house. Scarf nodded and answered, chuckling, 'Not all, but most of them. These walls are pretty thin.'"

Decka thought for a second. "I'll definitely think about asking her out, but I'm not sure she really likes me. I sound like an idiot when I talk to her, and she probably thinks I'm a weirdo."

Dear put her hoof on his shoulder. "Trust me, Decka, us girls know things, and she likes you."

"Well, I don't even have a lot of money to bring her somewhere nice she deserves." He started weighing the pros and cons. "I suppose I could cook her a nice dinner. Although, I don't even know what she likes to eat. I guess I could ask before I cooked something to make sure."

He kept making reasons for and against until Bill the Penguin interjected, "Hey, it's just dinner, that's all. Even if you burn it, you can order a pizza."

That simple advice made all the difference in the world. Although he thought of one major hurdle that could be a huge problem.

"How am I going to explain any of this?"

It was clear he needed more answers.

Bill the Penguin waddled over to Decka and sat next to him. "What I was going to tell you before is even more important that I tell you now. I'm going to do my best to explain."

Decka listened closely.

"Part of the spirit that we have comes with certain, oh how do I say "benefits." So, the reason you can see and talk to me, Scarf, Dear, Rayne and everyone else that you'll eventually meet is because of the love of Christmas that you have in your heart. You question how this is possible, but not that it is actually real. It's because of the Christmas spirit that it is possible. It's also because of the Christmas spirit that we see things others can't see."

He paused for a minute. "Is any of this making any sense yet?"

Decka almost understood, but not quite yet. 'What do you mean by "See Things That Others Can't See"?'

Bill the Penguin giggled. "This is one of the two major things that's hard to get used to."

"So, the only ones that can see us are those who not only believe, but to them the feeling of Christmas just is. You see, Decka, you never made a conscious choice to believe. You just always had Christmas in your heart. Just like you never thought about having to breathe, you never thought about believing in Christmas. For the record, it makes us sad when someone doesn't believe in Christmas. We love for people to believe. But, I'm just talking about why you can see us and why we can see you."

"Is it making more sense now and other people that might visit? Say like a beautiful girl we hope you ask over for dinner."

Decka was starting to piece it together. "So, if Alicia comes over, she won't be able to see or hear you guys?"

Scarf, Dear, and Rayne all nodded in agreement. "That's right."

Bill the Penguin added, "And that goes for anyone else you invite over, too."

Decka took a moment to absorb this. "I mean, it's not ideal, but I understand. I just wish I could introduce you all to my friends. It's going to be a challenge to balance conversations and give everyone enough attention. But I'll do my best not to leave anyone out."

"We're not concerned about that," Dear reassured him.

"Yeah, we just wanted to make sure you were aware, especially if Alicia comes over. We wouldn't want it to be a shock for her," Rayne confirmed.

"Got it. Hey, Bill, you mentioned there were two major adjustments to get used to. What's the other one?" Decka asked curiously.

"Oh, this is the big one," Bill replied, preparing Decka for what was to come. "It might be a bit of a shock at first, but I promise it's nothing to worry about.

Decka's apprehension grew. "Okay, what is it?"

"Alright, so you know how we talked about being who we want to be and what we want to be called?" Bill paused for Decka to acknowledge.

"Yeah, I remember."

"Well, it's not just us who get to be who we want to be," Bill continued. "Have you noticed how we're all at eye level with you?"

Decka glanced around, realizing the consistency in their heights. "Yeah, now that you mention it. But what does that mean?"

"It means that when we're all together, you get to be who you want to be too," Bill explained.

Confused, Decka replied, "I'm still just me, though."

Bill smiled knowingly. "You'll see. I think it's time."

Dear and Rayne walked over to a rectangular object that was covered with a blanket against a wall. Bill the Penguin grabbed Decka's hand with his wing and led him over to where they were all waiting. Decka could tell, standing in front of it, that it was a mirror.

"Are you ready?" Bill the Penguin asked.

Decka slowly shook his head up and down to signal Dear and Rayne to unveil what was behind the mirror. They both used one of their hoofs on each side to knock the covering off.

As the blanket fell, his eyes opened wider than his face was probably made for. He stood in awe at the reflection that was staring back at him. It wasn't that he didn't recognize the person he saw. As a matter of fact, he was very familiar with him. The person looking back at him was him. But somehow, he was eight years old again.

6
The Magic of Christmas

Illustration by Logan Herrington

"How?"

"Well, that's a good start. He's speaking," Scarf declared, relieved.

Decka looked at everyone and then back again at the mirror. He was still eight years old.

"But how?" he asked again.

"Honestly, we don't know how. We just assume it's the magic of Christmas. We get to be what we want, and most of the time, it's something that's in our hearts and minds," Dear answered.

"Eight years old must have been a good time in your life," Rayne added.

Bill chimed in, "Only we can see you this way. If someone like Jerry or Alicia comes over, they'll see the regular you."

Scarf remarked, "Not that this isn't the regular you. This is actually the more regular you, if you get what I mean."

"But am I really eight or twenty-five?" Decka asked.

"Ah, now that's the best question of all," Bill the Penguin replied, a cheerful glint in his eye. "There is no time counting...ever."

Rayne was happy to take it from here. "We don't even know what day or year it is. For us, it's always just a Christmas day."

"Yeah, and we are whoever we feel like being or looking like," Dear added.

"This is craaaaazy... but soooooooo cooool." Decka was still gazing at himself and touching his face to make sure everything felt real.

"So how come I'm still a human form, and you guys are...well, decorations?" He thought about how he should clarify that. "Not that you're not alive and all."

"I could be in human form whenever and if I want, Good Buddy," Bill answered. "Right now, this is what we feel like being." He continued, "Whatever our Christmas spirit makes us feel, is what we are at that moment."

"We know a girl named Rhonda who spent a year or two as a candle because she loved the smell of a Yankee Candle, Balsam and Cedar scent," Scarf said as an example. "Come to think of it, it was perfect because Rhonda could light up a room."

"This is awesome!" Decka declared. "Although I feel terrible about one thing."

"What's there to feel bad about" Rayne asked.

"Well, this is all amazing, but I feel bad that you're all secluded in the attic. It's decent sized for an attic, but you're all stuck in this one space."

Chuckling together, they all waited for someone to tell Decka.

Bill stepped up and announced to the team, "Who said the magic of Christmas only happened here in the attic?"

"We just always stayed up here, so we didn't make things complicated for you," he added.

Dear picked up where he left off, "Yeah, we can go downstairs and the whole house if you are okay with it."

"Really?" Decka asked.

Bill piped in again, "Yeah, Good Buddy, technically we can go anywhere in the world we want," he continued. "Of course, we can only see each other like now amongst our own eyes. But the sky's the limit."

"Well, in that case, what are we waiting for...let's decorate the whole house!" Decka declared out of excitement.

He opened the door leading back down to the ladder and gestured with his arm, inviting everyone into the main part of the house.

Bill raised his wing to put a brief pause on the procession. "Hey, man. Ya see all those boxes over there in the corner?" He pointed to a wall where boxes and boxes of Christmas decorations were neatly packed and stacked.

"Yes?" Decka replied, his tone questioning.

"Well, I think I already know the answer to this question but is it okay if everyone comes?" he asked.

Decka laughed and somehow knew what was just about to happen. "I could never say No, and besides, we're going to need all the help decorating the entire house, aren't we?"

"I like the way you think, Good Buddy."

Bill turned back towards the boxes and yelled, "OKAY, EVERYBODY...IT'S TIME TO DO WHAT WE DO BEST AND BRINGLE ON THE JINGLE FOR THE SAKE OF KRIS KRINGLE!"

In a happy and haunted Christmas fashion, each box jumped off the top of the other until there was only one box on the ground, separate from the others. Simultaneously, the tops of the boxes opened, and every single ornament in them started jumping up and out in glee. Most of them were dancing, happily running or walking toward the downstairs entrance. All the decorations he loved putting up all year, were alive!

One by one, they made their way past Decka, who had the widest smile on his face. When they reached the ladder, they each found their unique way down from the attic to the main level of the house. He wasn't sure where they were all going, but he knew they would find the spot where they wanted to be.

It was July, but he loved seeing the decorations he'd collected through the years. A model resembling an Amusement Park Christmas scene wobbled as it made its way to the stairs, hopped down the ladder, and found a spot in the house. A ceramic, old-fashioned red truck with a Christmas tree in its bed drove by, ready to be displayed year-round. A knick-knack of three gingerbread men holding hands twisted past him, joyfully sticking together out in the wide open.

One of his personal favorite ornaments, Superman, flew by and even waved to Decka as he went. A flock of red cardinals followed the Man of Steel, soaring to somewhere in the southern part of the house. Even regular round ornaments rolled to their destinations somewhere in the home.

Decka was looking down the hole to the ladder of the attic and was about to go down when he heard something stomping toward him. It was a very frightening sound, and he was afraid to turn around to see what it was. The slow and methodical steps were getting closer and closer. Decka was frozen and could not bring himself to turn around to face this "could be" monster.

Suddenly, the sound and loud stomps stopped. Could the monster be gone? He wasn't ready to find out just yet.

There was a tap on his shoulder. "Oh no!" Decka actually whispered out loud. The thing behind him was not only getting closer, but it was directly behind him. Maybe if he ignored it, it would go away. There was a second tap on his shoulder. He thought that even if he looked like he was twenty-five again, he probably wouldn't have a chance of survival, let alone looking like an eight-year-old. However, he had no choice but to turn around and face whatever mammoth of a beast this could be.

At the speed of a sloth, he turned to face the shoulder tapper. It was his Christmas tree. It started hopping up and down on its trunk, and Decka realized that was the sound of the stomping. The branches were still folded in as it was put away last January in its tree bag. It stopped hopping and then opened a couple of its branches in the same shape of someone extending their arms wide out. The tree gently leaned forward and hugged Decka, using its branches to embrace him.

In just a few moments, Decka went from being scared to realizing he had just found a new friend. The Christmas tree scrunched back up to make itself thin enough to hop down and out of the attic. Decka decided it was time to follow and see what was going on downstairs himself.

He made his way down the ladder and was astonished by everything. Every single Christmas item from the attic was busily setting itself up or helping to arrange something else. He could see different rooms from the hallway in which he stood and didn't know which one to go in first. It was so overwhelming in the best of ways. He was close to the bathroom and caught his own eight-year-old glance in the mirror once again. He believed it, but wanted to double check this was still real. It was.

Decka noticed that Bill, Scarf, Rayne, and Dear were helping as well. He was so fixed on the parade of Christmas items going by in the attic, he never noticed that they had come down on their own. Bill walked over to Decka and said, "Hey there. Sorry, I should have warned you about "Fraser."

"Fraser?" Decka asked.

"The Christmas tree," Bill replied. "He can be intimidating at first, but he really is a sweetheart."

Decka laughed and said, "Just a bit, and I didn't see him coming at first." He continued, "Luckily, we hugged it out!"

In just a few moments that the two were talking, everyone was doing their part. Decka could see the final stages of the tree being done as Superman flew, spiraling around the branches, placing the lights perfectly. The red cardinals soared in a similar pattern, adding sparkling garland to Fraser for the finishing touches.

Everything was perfect.

Almost.

Decka noticed something missing. Something very significant. He had to let someone know, and soon.

"Hold on! Something is missing!" he announced in a worrying panic.

While he was in the living room, everyone in the house heard him and instantly stopped what they were doing.

Decka looked to the top of the tree. "The angel is missing!"

He felt sad that not only was the angel missing from the tree, but somehow with all the excitement, he somehow forgot about her. The angel was the same angel his mother and father used on their tree.

Dear walked up to Decka and lifted her hoof into his hand. "We know she's special to you for many reasons."

"One reason is because your parents are no longer here, and it's one of the few things you still have of theirs," she said empathetically.

Decka nodded. "Yes."

Scarf waddled over and took his other hand with his stick hand. "Well, you still have them and that memory, my friend."

He continued, "Ya see, the last thing we always do—and just like you said because she is so special—is wait until everything is all set up."

Rayne joined in, "And saving the best for last, she is the last thing to put on top of the Christmas tree."

The lights dimmed. Decka didn't have the attention span at this point to be surprised that a Christmas decoration just turned down the lights, but with everything else happening, it didn't matter.

A light blared toward the attic stairs. Decka turned his head to see the light on the front of the Polar Express Engine, which was aiming perfectly so no-one would miss the entrance.

Bells chimed, horns sweetly bellowed, and the most beautiful voice he had ever heard came down from the attic:

O Christmas tree, O Christmas tree, how lovely are your branches! O Christmas tree, O Christmas tree, how lovely are your branches! Not only green in summer's heat but also winter's snow and sleet. O Christmas tree, O Christmas tree, how lovely are your branches!

The only Christmas treetop he had ever known floated down from the attic as she continued to sing.

O Christmas tree, O Christmas tree, Of all the trees most lovely. O Christmas tree, O Christmas tree, Of all the trees most lovely. Each year you bring to us delight with brightly shining Christmas light! O Christmas tree, O Christmas tree, of all the trees most lovely.

She glided gracefully over toward the tree and gently lowered herself onto the top of Fraser.

The Christmas decorating was now complete.

Decka looked all around at his perfectly decorated surroundings and declared out loud. "This was the perfect weekend and night."

"I'm going to sleep so peacefully tonight, but man, tomorrow is Monday, and it's going to be tough to get up and go to work tomorrow," Decka mused aloud. "I wish I could stay home, but I need the money so bad. Maybe now more than ever."

He wished everyone a good night, laid down in his bed, and pulled the Christmas blankets up that his new friends from the attic had set for him.

7
Little Snowy White Lies

Illustration by Makenzie Evans

M onday morning had come.

"Oh, the weather outside is frightful, but the fire is so delightful. And since we've no place to go, let it snow, let it snow, let it snow."

Decka slowly opened his sleepy eyes to the sounds of Dean Martin playing on the radio. His mind was in an early morning fog, and he wasn't sure about anything yet. For a split second, he thought it was actually Christmas. Slowly coming out of the haze, he knew it technically wasn't, but he remembered everything that had occurred the last few days. It was still early July, as a matter of fact. Things were quickly becoming even more clear, and he realized it was morning. A quick glance at the clock and panic instantly kicked in.

"Seven forty-five!" he shouted. "I need to be at work in fifteen minutes and the drive is twenty minutes if I'm lucky to not get any red lights."

Decka jumped out of bed and ran to his closet. He grabbed a button-up shirt, which he immediately tossed on the ground due to the endless number of wrinkles it had on it. The second and only other choice was a navy-blue polo shirt. It was also very wrinkled but would show less when tucked into his also fairly wrinkled khakis. He didn't have time for fashion sense as he threw on socks and slipped into his shoes within record-breaking time. As he was about to run into the kitchen, he stopped for a millisecond and glanced at himself in the mirror. He was still eight, wearing adult clothes. He quickly looked down and still hadn't figured out how the clothes he wore changed size. Then again, he had already decided not to question the magic.

He dashed through the kitchen where Scarf and Bill were sitting at the table.

"Good morning, Decka!" greeted Scarf. "I hope you don't mind, but I changed your alarm setting from that annoying ringing to playing random Christmas songs."

Decka made a straight line to his wallet and keys. "Nope, loved it, man."

Talking and walking, he added, "Hey, I gotta go, I'm already late. Obviously, do whatever you guys want, and I'll see you later."

Bill got up from the table and, with his wing, quickly handed Decka a travel mug. "Here, Good Buddy, we would have made more of a breakfast, but you didn't have much food in here."

Decka smelled the top of the mug and asked, "Is this hot cocoa?"

"Yup, I found it in the back of the closet. Hope that's okay?" Scarf asked.

Smiling, Decka replied, "It's perfect!"

He opened the front door and shouted as he headed out, "See you guys tonight."

Opening his car door, he heard, "Who were you just talking to, D-Man?"

It was Jerry who was outside, watering his lawn. Running late, he said the first thing that came to his mind. "Oh, sorry, man, I'm super late, and I was just talking to myself."

He shut the door at the same time he was turning the key in the ignition. He realized what he said made no sense since he said, "See you *guys* tonight." And if he was talking to himself, it wouldn't be in the plural. Either way, he didn't have time for making up logic. He backed out of the driveway and headed to his job, hoping he wouldn't be too late. Jerry watched as he drove off, scratching his head.

Decka made it to work in record time but was still twenty minutes late. He hoped nobody would notice. More specifically, his boss. He was hardly ever late, but the corporate office he worked at gave little room to be human for the occasional life un-expectancies. A few months back, they fired a mom who was often late due to her child's special needs. They had told her it was not fair to everyone else who worked there. He always thought it was a weird thing to say, considering they never asked the employees. Decka was certain nobody would have cared.

Decka grabbed his travel mug and speed-walked into the building. The elevator was ready, and luckily, he was able to make it to his cubicle without anyone seeming to notice.

He logged onto his computer and before he could blink twice, saw an instant chat message blinking in the corner of his screen. He opened it and saw it was from his manager, Edna.

It read: "Please come see me when you have a moment."

"Crap." He knew what this was about.

There was no point in waiting, so he immediately got up and went into her office with his travel mug still in his hand.

"You want to see me?" he asked as if it was just seconds ago that he got the message.

"Yes Derek," Edna replied. "Can you just close the door?"

He shut the door and turned back toward his manager.

Edna's expression twisted into an arrogant smirk as she spoke, her voice taking on a robotic tone. "I noticed you were late this morning," she stated, relishing the chance to engage in this conversation. "I know you are hardly ever late, but I still need to make sure I do my job and let you know I noticed."

In his head, Decka said, "*Yeah, I bet you can't even think of another time I was late.*"

The boss wasn't done. "Just please don't be late again so this doesn't become a bigger issue."

He was still talking in his own head and wondered if she could read it. *If it's not an issue, then why am I standing here listening to you.*

She couldn't read his mind, or she would have known the answer to what she was about to ask.

"Can I ask you why you were late anyway, Derek?"

He wanted to say that he overslept because he had the most comfortable sleep-in ages. He wanted to brag that he felt like he slept in the clouds last night. That his blankets and pillow felt like they were made in the North Pole. His dreams were filled with elves, friends, family, and everyone and everything he loved. He wanted to tell her that he could be listening to Elvis Christmas classics with Scarf right now. He could be sitting on the floor in between Rayne and Dear, watching the train roll around the bottom of a smiling Fraser. He wanted to tell Edna that Bill could be telling him more about Santa and all the magic of the season that he's still yet to learn.

But instead, he needed to answer to this person who was deemed responsible for hitting the enter button and all so his timecard would be sent to payroll for a paycheck that was barely paying to keep the roof over his head.

"I'm sorry, I must have somehow forgotten to put my alarm clock on after the long holiday weekend," he told his second fib already that morning.

Edna had to get one last shot in. "Well, don't let it become a habit," she remarked, her tone dripping with condescension.

"I won't, and thank you," he replied. He wondered why he thanked her for being condescending.

He thought the conversation was over, so he turned to leave, but before he reached the doorknob, she had one last question. "Derek, is that hot chocolate you're drinking in July?" she asked, her tone incredulous.

Now he really wished she could read his mind so she would have heard, "*Since when is what I'm drinking in the morning any of your business, Scrooge-Lady?*" Scrooge probably wasn't the right description since most people who worked for the company barely made any money, including the managers.

"Yes, I was so worried about getting here that I guess I blindly grabbed it, trying to get here so fast."

That was the third lie of the day.

"Okay, then. It smells amazing," Edna said.

Anyone else, Decka would have shared and poured a little in their cup. But not after this meeting.

He hoped Santa wasn't watching when he smiled and replied, "It sure is!" He took a big sip and finally walked out the door. This was the best hot chocolate he'd ever had. He couldn't wait to thank Scarf and ask how he made it taste so good.

The rest of his workday was just as unfulfilling as usual. He was responsible for running and creating reports for the company. Most of it, he didn't even care or bother to understand. The one thing he knew for sure was that the company was making lots of money, and none of it was for the workers. The company would have occasional meetings where the higher-ups would brag about double and triple-digit earnings. Yet when it came to raises, almost everyone got small percentages of the earnings.

Every day, Decka couldn't wait to go home. Now, with his new house buddies, waiting to go home seemed like an eternity. He thought if most people wait 365 days every year for Christmas, then the equivalent for him might be 3,365 or maybe even 33,365 days. His brain was thinking random and nonsensical things, waiting for the clock to move.

He already had his keys in his hand and was going to leave the building as quickly as he entered it that morning. Finally, five o'clock hit and it was time to head home. He jumped up out of his chair, grabbed his travel mug and darted toward the elevator. He was debating taking the stairs. For one, it might be faster. For a second, what if the elevator got stuck. He didn't need a third reason and decided the stairs were the best decision. He put his hand on the door when he heard the most awful sounds.

Edna's cringing voice.

"Derek. I saw you leaving, and I'm sorry. Company rules." She was standing in between the doorframe to her office, almost like she was doing security. "You need to make up the twenty minutes you were late."

He hadn't even turned around yet, which was convenient, so his manager couldn't see his eyes roll. For a split second, he wanted to just keep pushing the door that his hand was still on. Decka knew he couldn't. He had too many bills and was struggling financially as it was. He looked down at this travel mug and thought about Scarf and everyone else at home. He had to do all he could to keep things as they were at home.

Decka turned around and slowly made his way back to his cubicle. He passed close to Edna and decided to unleash another untruth. "I'm so sorry, I wasn't even thinking. Just a habit to leave at five."

She just nodded and looked at his shirt and khakis up and down. It was her subtle way of letting him know she noticed his wrinkled clothes.

He somehow knew she was dying to get that in too.

Decka sat back down at his desk and pretended to work on another report. What he was really doing for the next twenty minutes was wondering if Scarf had some magical powers to make an un-meltable snowball in the middle of summer that he could toss at Edna.

As soon as the twenty minutes were up, he left as quickly as he had tried to a few moments prior.

This time, nobody stopped him, and he was in his car and on his way back home. He thought about what he should have for dinner and then wondered if his new friends ate food? He quickly realized that was nonsense and just had to worry about what he was going to eat. Since it was just him, it would be the usual cost-cutting dinner. Ramen Noodles.

He pulled into the driveway and got out of the car when Alicia was just coming down the sidewalk. She was holding a blue leash and walking a yellow Labrador Retriever. Decka walked to the foot of his driveway just in time to greet the strollers.

"Well, hello," he said to both Alicia and her furry friend. "Can I pet him or her?"

"Of course," she replied. "It's a him. His name is Barney."

"Well, hey there, Barney." He got down on his knee and patted his head.

"Are you just getting home from work?" she asked.

"I am, how about you?" he asked and then rephrased. "Assuming you had to also go to work today?"

"Unfortunately," Alicia said, sighing. "Got to pay those bills and buy this guy food."

"I hear ya on that," Decka answered, his mind briefly drifting to his own financial struggles. He wanted to ask her out but didn't have the courage. He wanted to keep talking but didn't know what to talk to her about. Finally, the only thing he could think of was, "Well, if you ever need someone to walk Barney, don't hesitate to ask."

"I might take you up on that," she replied with a smile. "Well, have a good rest of your night." With a wave, she turned and strolled back down the sidewalk toward her house just down the street.

Decka entered his house to find all the Christmas decorations facing the window where he had just been talking to Alicia. "Were you guys all listening to my conversation?" he asked, half-amused and half-embarrassed.

Suddenly, they all moved away, returning to their original positions from earlier that day. All except Bill, who waddled up to Decka. "Hey, Good Buddy, when are you going to ask her out?" he inquired with a twinkle in his eye.

"I don't even know if she would say yes, and besides, even if I could, I don't have any money to take her out," Decka admitted, his tone tinged with disappointment.

Bill's expression softened. "Gee, we didn't even realize it was that bad, Decka," he responded sympathetically.

Decka walked over to a pile of mail that had come through the mail slot in the door earlier in the day. "I bet the mailman delivered some late bill notifications today." He looked through the envelopes and pulled two out. "Yup, here are two. The water and electric bill."

He looked up at the ceiling and then over toward the bathroom. "Well, the lights are still on and the toilet still flushes, so we're good if we're a few days late."

Rayne had since walked over and heard the conversation. "I know this doesn't help, but any of us that actually light up don't use the kind of energy that utility companies charge for."

Decka smiled and patted Rayne's head as he had just done with Barney. "That does make me feel better. Thanks." He felt the need to add, "And even if they charged me double, I wouldn't let them shut anybody off around here."

Dear came galloping in from another room. "Hey sorry, we all kind of heard that whole conversation about electricity and lights and stuff." Something was brewing in her head. "Would it be okay if tomorrow we decorated the outside of the house?"

Decka didn't even need to think about the response. "Well, my neighbors are going to think it's a little strange, but who cares? Go for it!"

Dear whistled and looked around to make an announcement. "LISTEN UP EVERY-BODY TOMORROW IS OUTSIDE DECORATING DAY!"

The whole house applauded as if everyone's favorite team won the Super Bowl.

"One question, though," Decka stopped to ask anyone who would answer, "How will Jerry or anyone not see you?"

Scarf put his stick hand up in the air to answer. "That's easy. First, Jerry is retired, so he takes a two-hour nap every day at one and second, during the work week, hardly anyone drives by anyway."

Bill added one last reason, "There's also that thing where they can't see us because the feeling of believing just isn't in them."

Decka was ready to eat. He woofed his Ramen noodles down in the kitchen without even sitting down. When he was done, he walked into the living room and looked out the window down the street toward Alicia's house. Maybe he could figure out how to get a little overtime at work and make a little extra money to cook her a nice dinner one night soon. He remembered how his morning started and that he didn't even have time to shower. He hoped Alicia didn't think he smelled. If she did smell something, maybe she thought it was Barney. He laughed to himself at the random doubts.

It was still early, but it was a long day and he felt himself getting tired. The money was the only stress he had, but it was still weighing on him. Decka caught his eight-year-old reflection in the windowpane. Although he looked young around his new friends, on the inside, he felt old again. Even older than he really was.

He was still looking out the window when he felt a prickly but comforting arm around his shoulder. He looked up, and it was Fraser. Even though Fraser didn't talk, he somehow knew Decka needed a bud right now.

Decka looked up at the top of the tree and saw the angel looking down.

She smiled so peacefully that it was warm and soothing. "Is it okay if I just call you Angel?" Decka asked. She smiled and winked back, and he knew that was a yes. He thought he even saw something sparkle in her eye when she winked.

Turning to everyone, Decka announced that he was going to bed, hoping to rise and head to work a bit earlier the next morning. They all bid him good night, and before he even stepped out of the living room, the Angel began singing the perfect bedtime lullaby, her enchanting voice wrapping around Decka like a comforting embrace from above.

"Silent night, holy night! All is calm, all is bright, round yon virgin mother and child. Holy infant, so tender and mild, sleep in heavenly peace. Sleep in heavenly peace."

Decka pulled his blankets over himself as he felt his eyelids grow heavy. The stresses of the day melted away as he surrendered to the peaceful music. With the comforting sound of the lullaby echoing in his ears, Decka drifted off to sleep, carried away by the wings of the Angel's voice.

8
$15.82

Illustration by Jennifer Perry

Decka was "up and at 'em" the next day. He took a proper shower and was even able to iron a couple things for work. Like the day before he had a cup of hot chocolate waiting for him, made by Scarf. Somehow, without even rushing, he was able to get out the door an extra hour early. The sun hadn't even fully risen yet, and he had to turn on his headlights in the car.

He arrived at work forty-five minutes early and hoped Edna wouldn't complain about having to pay for just a few extra hours. In fact, he also hoped she would forget about his tardiness from the previous day. Within the next hour, his coworkers arrived along with Edna. Nobody said anything about Decka being the only person sitting in a cube when they walked into the office. The morning proceeded without conversation regarding the extra hours. As time went on during the workday, Decka felt better and better that the overtime hours were going to be okay. He felt even better that he didn't really converse with Edna all day.

By the end of his shift, he was certain he could maintain this schedule for the rest of the week. With just a few additional hours he would have in his paycheck, Decka knew he was on his way to being able to buy enough decent food items to make Alicia a dinner she wouldn't at least laugh at.

On his way home that night, he thought about watching a movie. He couldn't decide which one, though. Thoughts ran into each other and he couldn't pick. He narrowed it down to four: *Elf, Miracle on 34th Street, It's a Wonderful Life,* or *Polar Express.* By the time he reached his street, he still hadn't decided on which one. He saw Alicia coming down the sidewalk with Barney just as they did yesterday. He turned into the driveway and was excited to meet them on the sidewalk again.

By the time he got out of the car and walked to the front of the sidewalk, he noticed they had stopped and were staring at the house. Before he caught what they were looking at, he remembered what he had somehow forgotten.

Bill, Rayne, Dear, Scarf, and everyone else said they were decorating the outside of the house that day. Decka was concentrating on Barney and Alicia and didn't even glance at his house when he pulled in.

He stared at the house himself and was astonished, just as Alicia seemed to be. Along the edges of the trim of the house were icicle string lights. The banisters on the front door were glimmering with silver and gold garland. The walkway had candy canes leading down the path. Every single small redbud tree he had in the front yard had ornaments hanging from it. Bushes aligned on one side of the yard were also laced with strings of lights.

During the star gazing that had been going on between Alicia and Decka, Jerry had wandered over. "It's a little early, D-Man, isn't it?" he said, chuckling.

Snapping out of his daze, "It's never too early bro."

"When did you do all this?" Alicia asked. "It wasn't like this yesterday, and aren't you just getting home from work?"

She had a good point and would need a good answer. Decka couldn't just tell her it was his living decorations in the house that they couldn't see. He would have to think of something else.

"Well, I couldn't sleep last night, and I needed to do something to try and make myself tired," he continued with his fib. "I guess I just kept going."

Jerry piped up, "I don't think I saw them this morning, though."

He had a good point, but Decka couldn't do anything except deny it. "They were definitely there this morning, I guess you just didn't think to look."

"Probably not." Jerry just laughed. "Well, I got burgers on the grill. After all, it still is summer." He laughed again and went back to his house.

Decka looked over to one of the front windows and could see everyone inside staring out. They all had wide grins on their faces. He could almost hear Bill giggling.

Alicia turned and looked at Decka and said, "Well, good for you!" She thought about what she was saying mid-thought and continued, "Well, not the not sleeping part, but putting up the Christmas decorations and not caring what people think."

Decka thought about how she could have made him feel like a weirdo, but she went with it and took the time to see his point of view. He loved that she had done that.

"Thank you for saying that." He realized he had not pet Barney yet and gave him an extra big pat and pet on the head. Barney wagged his tail excitedly and tried to lick his hand with appreciation.

He looked back toward the window and in unison, lips were mouthing the words "Ask Her Out." Decka wanted to but wasn't ready to just yet.

"Well, I should probably get in and get my things done, so maybe I can catch some Z's tonight."

Alicia smiled, looked back at the house one last time and said, "Me too. I need to feed myself and good 'ole Barney." They wished each other a good night and parted.

Decka walked into the house and into a gang of disappointed faces who apparently moved from the window to the kitchen doorway with the mission of a lecture. Jerry's house was not the only place for grilling that evening. They took turns asking the same question, only in different ways.

Rayne pondered, "Why didn't you ask her?"

Dear pressed, "What are you waiting for, Decka?"

Bill inquired, "When are you going to ask her out?"

Scarf joined in, "How many times are you going to pass before you ask her out?"

Fraser, though silent, seemed to shrug, silently questioning, "What's the deal, Decka?"

Every other decoration seemed to question Decka's hesitancy by looking around and trying to get the answer from someone else.

Decka finally answered, "Hey, everyone. I just need another week. The OT I work this week will be in next week's paycheck, and then I'll ask her over for dinner."

He thought for a second. "And by the way, when I do, I expect no spooky stuff."

Bill reassured, "We promise, and besides, remember only you can see us." He added,

"Alicia enjoys Christmas, but she's not as devout a believer as just a select few people are nowadays, Good Buddy!"

That was good enough for Decka. He went into the bedroom to change his clothes. He saw himself in the mirror and again at his perfectly fit clothes for an eight-year-old. Laughing to himself, he dug into the bottom of one of his drawers and pulled out his Christmas pajamas. He pulled them on his now child-like body and marveled at the "snuggle-ness" of them.

"Okay, I have a question for you all now," Decka asked, walking into the living room. "What movies do we want to watch tonight?"

"Raise your hands, or whatever you can raise to vote." He polled the room, "*Elf, Miracle on 34th Street, It's a Wonderful Life,* or *Polar Express.*" As he went through each movie, Decka paused and took a count. "*Polar Express* wins!"

Dear raised her hoof, as if seeking permission to speak. "Decka, before we start the movie, we have to show you something," she said with a gentle tilt of her head.

"Actually, we have two things to show you," Scarf interjected, his voice carrying a hint of excitement.

"First is on the kitchen table," Dear chimed in, her voice filled with anticipation.

Decka walked over to the table and beheld a substantial pile of coins alongside a couple of crumpled-up dollar bills. "What is that, and where did you get it?" he asked, his brow furrowing in confusion.

"While you were changing into your PJs, we searched all over for lost pennies, nickels, dimes, and quarters in the house," Scarf explained, his tone animated.

"Yeah, we actually came up with a total of $15.82," Bill exclaimed, his voice booming with pride.

"In this house?" Decka questioned, disbelief evident in his tone.

"That's right, most of it was under the sofa cushions or beneath the furniture or washing machine, or wherever," Dear added, her voice carrying a touch of amusement.

"Superman even flew under the fridge and found a ten-dollar bill," Rayne chimed in, his tone playful.

"Not sure how I lost that one?" Decka scratched his head, his voice tinged with bewilderment.

"Now you might have enough to make Alicia that dinner you were talking about," Scarf stated, his voice filled with encouragement.

"Well, I guess I could make that work," Decka replied, still scratching his head, flabbergasted.

Dear had more to give Decka and came walking over with a piece of paper in her mouth. She placed it on the table. "I found this very inexpensive recipe for chicken and potatoes," she said, continuing, "You probably will even have enough for dessert. "A big smile came over Decka. "I can't believe it."

Bill exclaimed cheerfully, "Hey, Good Buddy, I don't think you have any excuses now!"

Decka looked at him. "I guess I don't." He said with excitement. "I'm going to ask her tomorrow."

Everyone cheered.

"Thank you, everyone!"

He thought for a moment.

"Wait, what was the other thing you wanted to show me?" he asked.

Dear answered. "Well, now that it's dark out, you get to really see how the outside looks."

The summer sun had just set. Decka walked out the kitchen door and made his way down the driveway. Before he even stepped a few feet, he could see an illumination coming from the front of the house.

His eyes lit up. Everything he had seen just a short time ago was now glowing like the most gorgeous stars he'd ever seen. The lights on the trees were twinkling, and the ornaments were swaying in the breeze. The most amazing part was the part he somehow failed to see when he was seeing it for the first time with Alicia. It was what was on the roof. A sleigh with Santa and the reindeer as if they had landed on the roof. There were lights underneath the display, which spotlighted each almost real-looking feature. On the sleigh itself was a word that was lit up in gold that anyone driving by could read easily. It read: "Believe."

Of course, he was already beyond the need for belief, and the spirit of Christmas had become ingrained within him. Yet, he loved the idea that perhaps he could remind everyone else to believe, or even to start believing. He gazed around, marveling at the sheer perfection of everything before him.

Decka finally went inside and didn't need to tell everyone how incredible everything was. It was all over his eight-year-old face.

"How did you get the Santa Claus and display, though?" he asked. "It's the one decoration I never had."

Bill waddled up and whispered, "Let's just say we have our ways and a few connections Good Buddy!"

Decka thanked everyone for a second time. "Before we start the movie, I want to do one thing really quick."

He felt his luck was at the highest it had been in a long time and wanted to take advantage of any good fortune he had. He found an old box of Christmas cards and grabbed one out of it. Decka picked up a pen and began to write in it.

Hi Alicia,

I hope this isn't too forward or makes things awkward for us, but I was wondering if you would like to come over for dinner on Saturday night? It won't be very fancy, so don't feel bad about saying no.

From Derek

For a second, he almost signed it, Decka, but remembered he should take things like that slow. Alicia probably already thought he was odd anyway, and he was just hoping for one little dinner with her.

He licked the envelope and walked down the sidewalk in his Christmas pajamas. Her house was only a few down, and it was dark out, so nobody would probably see him anyway. Not that he cared. Decka put the card on her windshield so he wouldn't startle her by putting it through the mail slot in her front door.

On his way back, he heard a voice, "Are you wearing Christmas pajamas D-Man?"

It was Jerry looking out his front window.

"Yup," Decka said matter-of-factly.

"Hey, I don't care about all the Christmas stuff, but just making sure you're feeling okay, D?" Jerry asked.

Decka knew he wasn't being sarcastic and was genuinely concerned for his friend, so he wanted to answer truthfully.

"Honestly Jerry, I've never been better!" he replied.

He walked back to his house and spent the rest of the night watching Polar Express with his friends. He spent half his brain watching the movie and the other half thinking about what Alicia would say.

The next day was almost a carbon copy of the day before, getting to work a little early and getting home around the same time. He thought about the letter he had written less than twenty-four hours earlier.

Right on schedule, he turned down his street and could see Alicia and Barney walking down the sidewalk at their usual pace. Just as the evening before, Decka strolled down the driveway to greet them both. Barney was wagging his tail and happily panting, eager to get his new daily pat on the head. Decka leaned down and rubbed the puppy's head.

Decka pondered, Should I ask right away? Nah. Instead, he opened with, "How was your day today?"

"Oh, the usual work stuff, nothing exciting," Alicia replied and continued, "This week is kind of dragging."

Internally, he thought, *Boy, you're not kidding. I've been wondering all day if you saw the letter.*

Alicia looked up at the house decorations and smiled. "I'm still not used to seeing Christmas lights in July, but it makes me smile, at least."

Inside his mind, he deliberated, *she hadn't mentioned the letter. Perhaps she didn't see it or doesn't want to come over, which I understand, and I'm definitely not going to press her on it.* He wondered if she could hear what he was thinking.

"Well, I gotta get Barney home. He needs a bath bad," she said, starting to walk away.

That seemed to settle it for Decka. He wasn't going to know either way.

"He smells okay to me," he said, laughing and petting Barney's head as a way of saying goodbye.

Decka started back toward his driveway, and Alicia began making her way down the driveway toward her house.

"Red or white?" a voice asked.

Decka wasn't facing anyone, but he quickly realized it was Alicia's voice. Turning back around, he saw she had only taken a few steps down the sidewalk.

"For Saturday?" she continued, "Would you prefer red or white wine?"

She got the letter! He thought.

"Oh, whichever one you think is perfect," he answered.

"Okay, what time then?" she asked.

"I'm home all day, so it doesn't matter if you've got something to do first," he replied.

"Nothing at all, either."

"Okay, how about six then?"

"Six it is."

"Well, have a good night again."

"You too!"

Alicia strolled down the sidewalk to her house, and Decka burst into his own house, his face beaming with joy. Once again, he sensed his buddies were listening in. Though he was certain they were all already aware, he couldn't contain his excitement as he proclaimed, "Dinner on Saturday, at six." The entire house erupted into applause, as if they had all just won the lottery. Well, a $15.82 lottery at that.

9
Dinner is Served

Illustration by Bryson Gross

The next day, Decka took his sofa lottery money to the store and bought all the ingredients that the recipe Dear had given him called for. She somehow also found a coupon that he was able to use to save an extra dollar. That came in handy, and he was able to buy a small apple pie and some vanilla ice cream.

Friday night, Decka had a small meeting with the family in which everyone agreed not to be spooky when Alicia was over. He knew she wouldn't be able to see them, but he could and didn't want to accidentally get caught saying something and having her think he was talking to ghosts.

Saturday night had come. Decka was a little nervous. He knew she thought the Christmas lights on the outside of the house were strange, so what would she think of the inside looking the same?

He looked at himself in the mirror a few extra times to check his face. He was seeing himself as an adult at the moment and wondered if it had to do with being nervous. He gazed at the clock and it was almost 6:00. Decka didn't have time to analyze it.

Ding Dong!

It was 5:55, and Alicia was here.

Decka looked around and whispered, "Okay, everyone, we'll chat in a few hours. Aaaaaand remember noooooooooooooo funny stuff!"

All the decorations went to a shelf, mantle, countertop, etc. Some even jumped on Fraser. Decka looked to the side kitchen door and didn't see Alicia. He realized she must have rung the front doorbell. He opened the door and waved her in.

"Come on in," he said invitingly.

She had a bottle of wine in each hand. "Thanks again for asking." She handed him the bottles.

"Thank you for bringing these," he continued. "Come on, let's bring them in the kitchen and open them."

It was a modest-sized house, but the trip from the living room and into the kitchen ended up being a slow one. Amazed at all the decorations, Alicia barely moved her feet, almost trailing him. He noticed she wasn't behind him and almost seemed to lose her in the small home. He poked his head and saw her frozen in the hallway, gazing over the walls at all the Christmas decorations. For a second, he thought she was going to leave immediately.

"This is amazing." Alicia finally spoke after a long pause and forward movement toward the kitchen. Her eyes were fixed on Scarf, who had parked himself in a corner. Decka could see the life in Scarf's eyes and was doing the most amazing job of just standing perfectly still.

"I don't know why I didn't think you wouldn't decorate the inside of your house too." She was now staring at all the ornaments on Fraser." She got really close—almost eye to eye—to Superman, who was hanging from the tree. Decka somehow knew how bad the Man of Steel must have wanted to show off his flying skills. Despite the oddness of the situation, everything seemed to be going smoothly. She glanced up at the angel atop Fraser, then moved slowly around the house, her speech matching her pace, delivered with a similar slowness and an air of astonishment.

"She's the most beautiful angel I've seen."

"Thanks, I've had her since I was a little kid," Decka said the word 'kid', which made him quickly check his reflection shining off a wine glass he had grabbed. He was happy to see he appeared to look like an adult. He went on, "Actually, my mother had it before me. Been in my family for generations and I don't think they make them like that anymore." Decka was now also staring up at the angel and he somehow knew the Angel was touched by the nice things being said.

The night had just begun and Decka was relieved that she didn't run away the minute she walked through the door. Alicia wasn't judging him and started noticing he wasn't as nervous anymore. He glanced over at his reflection in a nearby mirror, and he looked like a little kid again. The acceptance by Alicia must have made him feel at ease, and he appeared as he felt—innocent and carefree, just like he was when he was a kid on Christmas.

Both Alicia and Decka continued looking at all the decorations until dinner was ready. They ate in his small dining room. Alicia caught Decka chuckling to himself and asked what he was laughing at. He explained to her that he had never actually eaten in the dining room before and that this was a first. That made her laugh, too, because she never had eaten in her own dining room either. She told him she would have to have him over for dinner so she could use hers. Decka loved the fact the night wasn't over yet, and he had already been invited to a future date with Alicia.

After dinner, they went into the living room and sat on the couch. Alicia was gazing at Fraser when she turned to Decka and asked, "So, why do you like Christmas so much?"

He could tell she was not asking in a condescending way and was being sincere. Decka explained to her how much he loved the feeling he had when he was a kid and how it never went away as an adult. He explained how bad he felt when his parents would pack everything up and put it in the attic and how long the eleven months would feel. He really wanted to tell her how the decorations in the house could make her feel the same if they would just come alive and if she could somehow see them. He kept it basic for now.

Decka really wanted to tell her the story about Santa and how he was supposed to see something in the sky that night, but blew it by being sick. When he was done with his explanation, it probably was a good fifteen-minute speech. He realized he had gone on awhile and was probably making Alicia regret her question.

"I'm really sorry, I got carried away there," he went on. "I guess I should have just said, I wished the spirit that seems to be in people's hearts for just a few weeks at Christmas could be there all the time. I honestly don't know what makes people lose it."

"I love hearing you talk about it, and you don't need to apologize for telling me all that," Alicia responded. "You actually make me want to love it more than I do."

She went on, "I mean, I love Christmas, but I guess like everyone else with work and stress and all the adult things life throws at us, we don't have time to stop and enjoy things like we should."

Decka understood what she was saying and wished he could help her take away any stress she had, and silently wished one day he might get the chance.

Alicia looked at her watch and realized it was starting to get late. "I really should go home. Barney probably needs to go out and go pee."

"Let me walk you home, at least," he offered.

"Sounds good," she agreed.

They strolled down the sidewalk towards Alicia's house, the streetlamps casting a soft glow around them.

"Thank you so much for tonight," Alicia expressed her gratitude.

"No, really, thank you for coming and being okay with all the Christmas stuff," Decka replied sincerely.

"I still think it's a little weird, and although I won't be putting my tree up for a few months, I understand why you did it, and I like it."

"Well, have a good night and see you soon."

He anticipated Alicia to bid him goodnight, but instead, she surprised him with a kiss on the cheek, turning the already great night into something perfect.

Barney's barks pierced the quiet night. "I better go let him out before he has an accident," Alicia said, breaking the silence.

"Okay, good night again," Decka bid farewell and started his journey back home.

He was nearing Jerry's house when he heard Alicia call out to him, "HEY, DEREK!"

Turning around, he saw Alicia smiling and waving. "MERRY CHRISTMAS!" she exclaimed.

Whatever the word for "more perfect" is, it is how the night went.

10
IF MONEY GREW ON CHRISTMAS TREES

Illustration by Tracy Jones & Kelly Rankin

The next few weeks went by splendidly with Alicia and Decka seeing each other on the weekends with mostly the same kind of dinner dates. It was perfect especially for Decka, who was having a very difficult time making bill payments. It seemed like almost every day a late bill reminder would arrive in the mail. It was getting so bad, he realized he could never catch up even by working overtime. For this reason, he ended up spending any extra money he had on his dates with Alicia.

For the most part, the dates would alternate between Alicia and Decka's house. When at Decka's house, he always laughed to himself because he would occasionally catch a glance of his image in something and notice his younger image of himself, which looked strange next to an adult-looking Alicia. While Christmas made him feel young, as reflected in his mirror image, getting to know Alicia increasingly made him feel comfortable.

Occasionally, she would catch him staring at the mirror or at one of his hidden friends. She would ask, "What are you looking at?"

"Oh, sorry, uh...I was just daydreaming, I guess," he would reply, snapping out of it. How he wished she could see and talk to everyone that was surrounding her. It was almost unfair he got to enjoy the magic all by himself. There was a lot he wished he could tell her. Like that he wanted to be called Decka and not Derek. The only small thing he found amusing was the mistletoe that would just wondrously show up above them, so he could steal another kiss.

"How are you doing that?" She would giggle and peck Decka on the lips.

He would simply reply, "A magician cannot reveal his secrets."

Whenever Alicia left, he would bring it up. "Misty, one of these days, she's going to catch on." he laughed, knowing it was impossible.

Misty the Mistletoe just giggled and found another door frame to hang from.

Weeks passed in a repetitive cycle, with days blending into one another. Then, on a mid-October night, Decka made a decision that would prove unpopular within the family.

One night while hanging out at Decka's again, Alicia mentioned how she felt bad about leaving Barney because he seemed to be not feeling well. Of course, Decka would not have minded going to her house. However, he had already started cooking dinner. He of course, was worried about Barney also and said, "Well, I don't mind if you want to bring him over here so we can keep an eye on him."

"Are you sure?" Alicia asked. "I'll be worried if he gets sick and we can't get him outside in time." Derek laughed and said, "It's okay, it's not like I have anything valuable in here."

He saw out of the corner of his eyes that Bill, Scarf, Dear, Rayne, and everyone else didn't like that comment. They were all simultaneously shaking their heads. He would have to clarify that one later.

"Well, if it's really okay, I'm going to go grab him quick," she said, glancing at Decka for reassurance.

"I don't mind in the least bit," Derek reassured her with a smile.

Alicia hurried out the door to fetch Barney. As she dashed down the driveway, Bill, Scarf, Dear, and Rayne gathered around Decka.

"Okay, I'm sorry, guys. I didn't mean to imply you weren't valuable. I was talking about the rugs and floor and things," Decka attempted to clarify, sensing their unease.

Bill chimed in, "That's not what we were shaking our heads about, either."

Scarf added, "Yeah, we're not big fans of dogs."

Bill nodded in agreement, "Yeah, I mean, we like them, but they don't always like us back."

Rayne interjected, "Just ask Fraser how many times he's been peed on." They all glanced sympathetically at Fraser, who was shaking himself vigorously.

"Oh man, I'm sorry, guys, I didn't even think," Decka apologized sincerely, realizing his oversight.

Suddenly, the side door opened with Alicia and Barney coming through. Bill, Scarf, Dear, and Rayne froze where they were standing in the kitchen. Alicia had a confused look on her face.

"Who were you just talking to, and why are these decorations suddenly just in here?"

Decka didn't know how he was going to get out of this one. He had to say something, even if it wasn't going to sound good. "Well, um, I was just going to move these few things to make more room for Barney so he can feel relaxed," he stammered, aware of how feeble his explanation sounded. Alicia squinted in confusion.

"Um, okay," she replied, her confusion evident in her tone.

Decka scrambled to think of a way to further clarify, but Barney chimed in and saved the day.

Bark! Bark! Bark!

Barney had made his way into the living room and was staring at Fraser. His barking was an excited bark. However, the circling and frantic tail wagging made Fraser shiver in fright. Alicia couldn't see, but Decka could see the look on Fraser.

"Wow, he must really like the tree." Alicia said jokingly.

"Yeah, he's a friendly pup and probably just wants to be friends," Decka said hoping Fraser would hear and it would calm his anxiety.

Decka almost forgot everyone else, who were just frozen in the middle of the kitchen. He quickly grabbed them and placed them in a backroom, where he closed the door. He thought to himself, well, four of them are safe. Barney started noticing other decorations and barked at them, too. The only one who didn't seem scared was Superman, but after all he was the Man of Steel and could fly away whenever he wanted. Moments passed, and Barney was now galloping and panting from room to room. If Barney were a cat, it would have been as if he had gotten the best batch of catnip ever. He was excited and happy.

"Well, I don't know what's gotten into him but I don't think he's feeling sick anymore." Alicia declared.

"Maybe he likes Christmas all year round too!" Decka replied.

Alicia wrapped her forearm around his. "I think I'm starting to, too!" Decka liked that.

They had dinner, opened a bottle of wine, and made their way into the living room to watch a movie. Barney had finally tuckered himself out and was lying on the tree skirt under Fraser. Decka could tell that Fraser was also comfortable and realized he never had a reason to fear Barney. If he didn't know better, he'd say they might be best new friends.

"It was getting late, and time for Alicia and Barney to go back home for the night. They kissed one more time under Misty the Mistletoe while Barney stared up and made a whimpering sound. They both laughed again.

"Let me guess, more magic?" Alicia asked.

Decka shrugged and said, "Hocus Pocus!"

They were all about to walk out the door when Barney turned back and made one last dash to the living room. He turned around, lifted his leg, and peed on Fraser.

"BARNEY!" Alicia scolded.

"Oh my God, I don't know why he just did that," she continued. "He knows to go outside. I'm so sorry. I'll clean it up." She started walking over to the paper towels.

"I got it," Decka replied. "It's really not a big deal." He hoped Fraser knew that he knew it was not a good thing."

Alicia threw Barney's leash around him and said, "Come on, you bad boy!"

They headed down the sidewalk to Alicia's house. Alicia ran into the house. "Hold on, I have something that'll help clean that up." She ran into her side door and before the screen door could close, she popped back out, holding a white bottle in her hand.

"This should work well on the tree." She handed the bottle to Decka.

"Thank you, I'll give it back tomorrow," he replied. "I loved having Barney over and am glad he seems to be feeling okay."

"Well, since we both enjoy coming over, if it's alright with you, I'll just bring him along more regularly," Alicia replied.

"You guys never need an invitation ever," Decka replied. "Goodnight again!"

He kissed her and went back home to clean up Fraser. He walked into the house and noticed the back door still closed. "IT'S SAFE TO COME OUT!" Decka declared.

The backdoor creaked open and Bill, Scarf, Dear, and Rayne's heads popped out stacked on top of each other. With a sigh of relief, they uniformly let out a "Wheeeeewww!"

"Okay, it wasn't that bad. He calmed down after a while," Decka said. He looked at Fraser and admitted, "Okay, well, except for that little incident at the end."

He started cleaning Fraser with the spray bottle Alicia had given him. After thoroughly wiping him down, he looked up at Fraser and said, "There, it's like nothing ever happened."

Decka continued, "Just giving everyone a heads-up, I told Alicia that she and Barney are welcome to come over whenever they want, which means to be prepared in case they drop in."

"Aye aye, captain...or Good Buddy!" Bill responded for everyone.

Decka's contemplative expression was evident as he mulled over something deeply.

"Got a question, Decka?" Rayne asked, noticing the thoughtful look on his face.

"Yeah." Decka replied absentmindedly, his hand unconsciously scratching his head. "Is it possible for someone to see you guys if they start truly believing?"

He was still grappling with how to articulate his thoughts. "You know, like if they weren't born with the feeling?" They all smiled knowingly before responding.

"That's an absolute Super-Yes!" Bill responded enthusiastically.

"The true feeling of Christmas is born within all of us," Rayne added, his voice carrying a warm reassurance. "Some, like you, are natural and have it always there without trying."

"And some have it, but lose it, and sadly never find it again," Scarf chimed in, his tone tinged with empathy.

"The really sad ones never find it at all, even though it's buried in their hearts," Bill lamented with a hint of sorrow.

"And once in a while, something happens where someone finds it and it explodes within them," Rayne stated optimistically.

"And it's one of the most beautiful things you'll ever see," Dear added, her voice carrying a gentle warmth. "Someone who finds the Christmas inside them that's always been there."

This sentiment struck a chord with Decka, filling him with a newfound sense of hope. As he pondered those words, his thoughts naturally drifted to Alicia. The image of her, her eyes bright with the joy of discovery, flashed through his mind. He couldn't help but feel a surge of optimism at the thought of Alicia embracing the magic of Christmas, finding within herself the same enchanting spirit that had captured his own heart. Maybe someday.

More weeks came, and so did more bills. It was now November, and each notice in the mail was more threatening. A few of his credit cards had even cut him off and informed him that he would be reported to credit bureaus. The stress was getting to him and he eventually had to tell Alicia about his financial issues. They had an honest relationship, and he thought it was important for her to know that he couldn't buy her nice things or take her to fancy restaurants. Alicia didn't care. She was not with Derek for his money but for how he went about the world. Like not caring about having Christmas decorations all year round. She had tried once to convince him to maybe cut down on the lights to save on the electric bill. But, of course, he wouldn't have it. The lights he had also didn't use additional utilities because they were powered by Christmas magic.

One night at work, Edna called Decka into the office. She had a more than usual serious look on her face. "Can you close the door?"

He sat down and waited for the point of this meeting. "Derek, this is hard for me to tell you, but I wanted to give you a heads up because you've been a good worker." Edna was serious.

"Nobody is going to hear this until after the first of the year, but we are going to be closing this office in January." She was genuine in her sadness at the bad news.

Decka was shocked and didn't even know what to say. "Why? We always seem to be busy and can't even seem to catch up?"

"The only thing I was told was they are moving this department overseas to save money," She answered, her brows furrowing in concern, while her shoulders slumped slightly, revealing her disappointment. "I won't have a job either."

"This sucks." Decka couldn't think of another way to describe what he'd just been told. He automatically thought about all the bills sitting unopened on his kitchen countertop and how he was even more in trouble now.

"I'm sure there'll be some kind of severance package, but of course, there aren't any details yet." Edna was talking while Decka was still processing. "Again, don't say anything, I'm only telling you and maybe a couple other people who I think deserve to know."

"Um, I won't." Decka's face fell, his expression mirroring the sensation of being punched in the stomach. "Well, it's the end of the day. I guess I'll see you tomorrow."

"Again, I'm sorry, Derek," Edna said with a sympathetic tone. "Tomorrow is Saturday, so I'll see you Monday."

Decka's shoulders slumped, and he managed a weak nod before turning away, his disappointment evident in the heaviness of his steps as he trudged out of the room.

He came out of his daze and realized she was correct. It was now the weekend. He grabbed the keys off his desk and made his way to his car. His mind was racing, thinking of every negative scenario all at once. Decka needed to think more, but he needed help thinking his way through this. He knew he needed beer and only had a couple of cans in the fridge. Although he really shouldn't buy anything, he felt so beyond help at this point. It didn't matter anymore. So he drove to the supermarket and bought himself the biggest pack he could find. He was determined to drink until he came up with the best economic plan ever. This was a terrible idea.

Decka pulled into his driveway and felt a deep sadness since he didn't see Alicia and Barney.

He thought about calling but didn't want to bother her with this gigantic new problem, so he didn't. He walked into the house, put the huge pack of beer next to the couch, and plopped down on the sofa.

"What's wrong, Good Buddy?" Bill asked.

Decka was looking down at his shoes and looked up to see everyone gathered around him. "Oh, nothing, guys," he replied. "Just some work stuff."

"Is it bad?" Bill asked.

"No, why do you ask?" Decka was lying but didn't feel the need to bring everyone down at the same time.

"Look!" Bill was pointing at a mirror on the wall.

Decka stood up from the couch and walked over to look. His image was old again. In a way, he thought he looked a little older than he was. He turned to everyone.

"Okay, I have a big adult problem that I don't know what I'm going to do about," he said while grabbing another beer. "These will help."

He sat there and drank the rest of the night away.

The next morning came, and he had never left the couch. He passed out and slept where he was. Like he'd done many times before, Scarf brought Decka a hot cup of coffee. "Thanks, bud, but these are all I want right now." He reached down in the box and found a can of beer.

Slurring, Decka muttered, "Even if they're warm, they're still good." He downed one beer within a couple of minutes and reached for a second. Surprisingly, it was only 9:00 AM.

He continued to sit and drink throughout the morning and into the afternoon. By the time it reached five o'clock...

"Derek?" someone called out.

"Derek?" It was repeated.

Alicia shook Decka's shoulder, asking, "Derek, are you okay?"

"Derek?" came the voice again, accompanied by a gentle shake of his shoulder. It was Alicia.

Decka mumbled incoherently, his bloodshot eyes meeting hers. "I think I drank a lot," he managed to say.

Alicia surveyed the scene, noting the scattered beer cans and the nearly empty box. "Well, considering there are beer cans all over the floor and this box is pretty empty, I'd say you did," she remarked.

Decka apologized, but Alicia reassured him, admitting she had never seen him in such a state before. She asked if everything was okay.

"Not at all. I'm being, um, fried," Decka replied, still struggling to articulate clearly.

"You got fried?" Alicia asked, shocked.

"Well, not fried, I mean fired," he clarified, still slurring. "We're being let go—sometime after the new year."

"Aww, that's awful," Alicia sympathized, beginning to understand his situation. "Hold on, I'm going to make you some coffee, and we can talk about it," she offered, heading towards the kitchen.

"I think Sharp, I—I mean Scarf, already made some this morning," he said, still slurring.

"Who is Scarf?" she asked, puzzled.

"You know, Scarf." Decka pointed to the snowman in the corner.

Scarf turned towards Decka. "Buddy, you know she can't see or hear us."

"No, man, just say hello," he replied.

"Who are you talking to?" Alicia was very confused.

"Scarf." He pointed again.

"Wow, you're really drunk," she said. "And where did you come up with that name?"

"I didn't, he named himself," Decka said. "Just like Bill, Rayne, Dear, Fraser, and everyone else."

"Derek, I really think we need to get you some coffee. You're not making any sense," Alicia said, walking into the kitchen.

Decka stood up and followed her. "No, they're all right here. Can't you see them? They're alive just like you and me."

"No, I just see a bunch of decorations, Derek," she answered matter-of-factly.

"I named myself too. Derek is okay, but my real name is Decka," he blurted out, courtesy of the beers he drank over the past 24 hours.

"Decka?" Alicia asked.

"Yeah, that's the name I named myself," Decka tried to communicate.

"Okay, I think after we get some coffee in you, we better get you some sleep too," Alicia suggested, trying to calm him down.

Despite his protestations, Alicia managed to coax him into bed, handing him a glass of water to drink. As she tucked him in, she promised to return with breakfast in the morning to discuss work.

As Alicia shut the door, Decka managed to mumble one last thing: "Alicia."

"I don't know what I'm going to do," he said, his voice sad and tired, but he managed to explain further. "Even if I can collect, it won't be a full paycheck, and I could lose the house."

"I'm sure things will work out," Alicia replied.

"If I lose the house, then I don't know how I'll be able to keep them safe." Decka tried to explain.

Alicia sensed he was serious, even though he was intoxicated. She didn't tell him he was imagining things. She just listened because it seemed to be coming from his heart.

"I'd hate to put them all in boxes with nowhere to go. That's not fair to them," he said under his breath as he drifted off to sleep.

"We'll talk more tomorrow," Alicia whispered. "Goodnight, Decka!"

She giggled, saying it.

The next morning came suddenly for Decka. The sun pierced through the window and lit his face like a spotlight. At first, he was confused about where he was. He looked around and realized he was in his bed, but didn't remember how he got there. He sat up, hoping it would help with clarity. Somehow, it did, and he started to recall the previous day's events.

"Oh no, I'm an idiot," he said out loud.

He walked into the kitchen where Scarf and Bill were sitting at the table. He grabbed a cup of coffee and sat down in front of them.

"I'm really sorry, guys. I guess I made a fool of myself the last couple of days."

"It's okay, Good Buddy. We all understand," Bill replied.

"Yeah, if we had jobs, we would have felt the same way." Scarf said.

Rayne and Dear came walking into the kitchen. "We all feel terrible that you're going through this, and we don't want to ever be a burden."

"A burden?" Decka said. "You're never a burden."

Scarf adding to the conversation. "Yeah, but if it wasn't for us, you wouldn't need to worry about keeping a roof over our heads."

Superman came flying in, "Yes, we are fine going back into storage somewhere if it means you have a place to stay."

"Listen, guys," Decka explained. "Nobody is going in storage anywhere. I'll somehow figure this out."

KNOCK, KNOCK!

Decka looked up and saw Alicia at the side door. He gave everyone a couple seconds to scatter and waved her in. She opened the door, and Barney was also there. Before he could even say anything, the puppy ran into the living room and lay at the feet of Fraser.

"Good morning," Decka said to Alicia with a look of embarrassment.

"How are you feeling this morning?" she asked.

"Surprisingly not too bad considering," he answered. "Coffee?"

"Sure." She replied.

"Here ya go." He put a freshly poured cup in front of her at the table.

Alicia giggled and asked, "Did Scarf make this?"

Her joking comment somehow brought the entire conversation back to his memory instantly. "Oh yeah, about that," Decka said.

"It's okay, I know it was the beer talking," she stated.

He was relieved that she was easily letting him off the hook. "Well, either way I'm sorry you had to see me like that, and thank you for making sure I got some water in my system before I passed out."

"It was really no big deal, and I understand," she reinforced. "Now, tell me about your job."

In a calm and much more coherent way, Decka told Alicia about his conversation with Edna and how the company was going in a different direction. He explained that there wasn't an exact date, but it seemed it was happening sometime after the new year. Decka also mentioned how he wasn't sure he could keep the house if he made less money because he was barely scraping by as it was. Alicia was surprised; she knew he didn't have a lot of money but didn't realize how much debt he truly was in. Knowing this made her even more concerned for him.

She said the only thing she could think of. "I'm sure we'll figure something out."

Decka wasn't convinced but liked the fact that she had said "we", even though it was his problem. The two talked for the next hour before Alicia noticed the time on the clock.

"Well, I need to run a couple errands, so we should probably go."

Decka peaked around the corner and noticed Barney started snoring while lying under Fraser. "I'm not sure he wants to go anywhere." He giggled.

"Unfortunately, I have to go to the mall to get someone at work a birthday present," Alicia said.

"Yeah, that's not a fun place to go at any time," Decka replied.

"I somehow was nominated to go pick up this gift that everyone pitched in for."

"Well, I can go with you if you don't mind the company."

"That actually just might make it more tolerable if you don't mind coming."

"I don't mind at all," Decka continued. "And if you want, Barney can keep sleeping away right there, and we can just come right back and get him after."

Alicia thought it was a great idea. "Sounds perfect."

They stood up, Decka grabbed his car keys, and left for the mall. They made their way to the department store where Alicia needed to go and picked up the present for her coworker. It was mid-November, and all the stores were dressed up for Christmas. Although Decka didn't love the rush and self-centered crowd that seemed to fill stores these days, he loved the feel of the music, lights, and displays. They bobbed and weaved through the mall and were close to the exit door to the parking lot when suddenly, Alicia tugged at Decka's hand and pulled him.

"Hey, hold on a sec!" She ran over to the front window of a toy store. "Oh my God, I haven't seen one of those in ages." She pointed at the toy in the middle of the display.

Decka laughed and asked, "Is that an Easy-Bake Oven?"

Alicia was still holding his hand and now pulled him inside the store. "Yup!" She dragged Decka down one aisle and then the next to find where they were stocked in the aisles. Finding them, she was surprised to see the range of products.

"I always wanted one when I was a child, but I never got it," she said, reminiscing. Decka could see that, for a moment, she was right back to being the age she was talking about. She looked over the different models.

"Wow, they've actually changed a lot," Alicia exclaimed, astonished. "Look, they have microwave versions, different bundles, and oh, look at all these pan accessories! Here's a pizza bundle!" She was going on almost like a small kid who was overstimulated by eating too much sugar. Decka couldn't help but smile at the joy she was showing. She stopped for a minute and turned to Decka.

"You know what, these are all great, but the one I wanted as a kid was much better." She started to describe it. "It looked like an actual oven and was pink with buttons." Again, Decka laughed to himself when she repeated that it looked like an actual oven.

"My best friend had one, and we'd make cookies, brownies, little English muffin pizzas, and quesadillas sometimes."

Decka loved seeing the child in Alicia come alive. He also knew immediately what he wanted to get her for Christmas. He was still holding her hand and asked. "Hey, it won't be from an Easy-Bake Oven, but how about some English muffins pizzas for lunch from my toaster oven?"

Alicia laughed. "That sounds perfect and yummy!"

They drove back to Decka's house and found that Barney was still sleeping in the same spot under Fraser. He didn't even raise his head to notice that they had come home.

"Wow, he really loves that spot," Alicia said.

Decka noticed Fraser was very comfortable too and wanted to say, "I think they're both very comfortable," but just shook his head in agreement.

They both spent the rest of the day and evening together. Eventually, it was time once again for Barney and Alicia to go home. Leaving was getting harder and harder for Decka. The minute he walked her down the sidewalk to her house, he started missing her. She wouldn't even be in the door before his heart started hurting.

On his way back, Decka spotted Jerry outside. "Hey, D-Man, how are you and Alicia doing?" he called out.

"Great, Jerry!" Decka replied with a smile.

"You guys make a great couple," Jerry remarked, his tone filled with genuine admiration.

"Thanks, I think I may have found the one." Decka couldn't believe that came out of his mouth so easily.

"Well, make sure you let her know," Jerry said, not knowing he was giving Decka some good advice.

"Definitely," Decka replied with a grateful grin. "Have a good night, Jerry!"

"'Night, man!" Jerry waved before heading back inside.

Decka went into the house and jumped on the internet. He needed to find an old vintage Easy-Bake Oven to give to Alicia for Christmas. He popped open his laptop and started a web search. He wasn't sure if his eyes popped or his mouth dropped open first, but he was shocked at the prices. At first, he thought he was mistaken. They're old and couldn't possibly be this much. But search after search resulted in the same. To his dismay, there was apparently a market for old Easy-Bake Ovens.

He searched for hours, looking through every eBay, used toy store, and marketplace site he could find. They were all similarly priced. He was so broke he wasn't sure how he could afford to get her one. He thought about what Jerry said. Although Jerry wasn't necessarily talking about buying her a missed Christmas present from her past, Decka knew that seeing the smile on her face when she got an Easy-Bake Oven for Christmas would be worth it.

Decka fell asleep on the couch while unsuccessfully trying to find a reasonably priced old vintage Easy-Bake Oven. He woke up to Scarf tapping on his shoulder with one stick hand and holding a cup of hot chocolate in the other. "Wake up, Decka, I think it's time for you to go to work."

Decka looked at the clock on the wall and realized he was late. He wasn't as late as he had been a few months ago when Edna made him stay late, but he somehow didn't care. He remembered what Edna had told him about his soon-to-be lack of employment the previous Friday and suddenly was not concerned about tardiness.

He grabbed the hot chocolate. "Thanks, Scarf." He took a sip. "I don't know how you make the best cocoa, but you do." He patted Scarf on his top hat.

Decka took his time getting ready and got to work when he did. He ended up being fifteen minutes late but didn't care. He thought, What are they going to do?

He could see Edna looking at him from her office. Decka stared at his messages, waiting to be called into her office, but the message never came. It was probably his body language walking in that told Edna it would not be worth the conversation.

For the next couple of hours, Decka just sat pondering his thoughts and thinking of ways that he could manage to buy Alicia's Easy-Bake Oven. He didn't have any savings, his credit cards were maxed, and he was pretty sure he couldn't get any overtime.

If only money grew on Christmas trees, he thought.

He was gawking at his email when the solution miraculously came through. He saw an email from the benefits department with the subject heading "Open Enrollment."

11
The Sweetest Present

Illustration by A.R.

He immediately knew where he could get the money. *I can borrow from my 401(K),* he thought. He had stopped contributing to his retirement plan a couple of years ago, but he had enough to borrow from. Decka knew that there would be tax penalties, but that was the furthest thing from his mind. All he cared about was seeing Alicia's smile on Christmas morning when she saw the Easy-Bake Oven.

Decka filled out the necessary forms to request the needed money. He even asked for a little extra for some breathing room. When he got home, he jumped on his laptop and ordered Alicia's present. He put it upstairs in the attic and couldn't wait for the time he could give it to her. But first, they had to get through Thanksgiving.

Thanksgiving arrived, and Alicia and Decka spent the entire day celebrating from morning till night. They began their day by preparing the turkey and side dishes together. Side by side on the couch, they watched the Macy's Thanksgiving Day Parade. Decka particularly enjoyed the parade's conclusion, when Santa made his grand entrance, marking the official start of the holiday season. He reflected on how, for most people, the holiday spirit only emerged at this time of year, unlike him, who carried it in his heart year-round.

Alicia liked the parade, but now had a new appreciation for it. She saw the extra glow in Decka's eyes when the man in red and Mrs. Claus came rolling down 34th Street.

"You're like a little kid," she said to Decka.

If she only knew, he thought to himself amusingly as he looked at his eight-year-old self in the mirror.

Thanksgiving passed, and now Christmas was coming. So did more bills.

Every day, overdue notices would arrive in the mail. He was so behind that Decka didn't even look at them. He would just grab the pile of envelopes and toss them on top of the kitchen counter without even opening them. There was no way he could catch up, so he just ignored them.

One letter that Decka never saw was a notice from the mortgage company. It was the first letter telling Decka that he hadn't made his monthly payment. He had paid what he could, but it was not the full payment due.

December 25th arrived, Alicia and Decka woke up together on Christmas morning. The night before Christmas Eve, Decka finally asked Alicia how she felt about spending

Christmas morning together.

"I thought you'd never ask," Alicia exclaimed. "Of course, Barney would need to stay over, too?"

"You know I love having him here," Decka replied, thinking how Fraser was going to enjoy having his buddy over, too.

Decka arranged with Bill and Scarf to place the Easy-Bake Oven in front of the tree, so it would immediately be seen by Alicia when she walked into the living room.

The morning arrived, and although it was freezing outside, the living room was warm and cozy with the glowing fireplace Rayne and Dear had prepared. It was just another perfect scene on Christmas morning.

Decka and Alicia took their time getting up but knew they couldn't stay in the comfortable bed all day. Decka waited for Alicia to get up first. She eventually sat up and stretched her arms in the air. "I think I'll go make us some coffee."

She walked out of the bedroom and turned toward the kitchen. Before taking one step in that direction, her head immediately snapped into the path of the living room. There, sitting in the perfect light, was a pink vintage Easy-Bake Oven. She slowly turned back to Decka, who was sitting up in bed, loving the sight of her surprise.

"Merry Christmas, Alicia!" he wished her.

Her eyes widened, and her mouth dropped open. She didn't speak for what seemed like hours because she wasn't sure what to say. Eyes welling up, she finally managed to say something.

"That's the sweetest present I've ever gotten." She walked back to Decka who was still sitting in bed, and hugged and kissed him on the cheek. Her embrace was as tight as he had ever felt from her. Decka was so happy that she liked it as much as he hoped she would.

Alicia lifted her head from Decka's shoulder and said, "If you make coffee, I'll make us cookies!" She, of course, was referring to baking a batch in her new oven.

"Sounds like a deal!" he replied.

He went into the kitchen and put a pot on. Scarf had already made a batch of hot chocolate too. As the pot was brewing, he saw Alicia playing with her Christmas gift. For a second, he saw a flash of her as an eight-year-old girl. He rubbed his eyes, and the gorgeous adult woman he had fallen in love with was back. Did he see for a brief second what he thought he saw?

He asked her, "I made coffee, but I also made some hot chocolate if you want that."

"Oh, hot chocolate for sure!" she replied.

He handed her a cup, and she took a sip. Her eyes closed in almost a dream sequence. "Okay, this is the best hot cocoa I've ever had in my life."

Decka knew that was true. After all, Scarf made it. A quick look over at Scarf, and he was smiling as if he knew it was the best hot chocolate ever too.

12
Unwrapping the Truth

Illustration by Alicia Greenlee

F ireworks, champagne, and watching the ball from Times Square on TV ushered in a new year.

While most people started taking down the Christmas displays and decorations, Decka kept them lit with no plan to ever take them down. The season of carols, holly, and jingling bells was never going to end again. He still felt terrible that he stored everyone up in the attic and vowed never to do that again.

A few weeks into the new year, Decka's employer announced that there would be a company-wide meeting on the Friday of that week. His coworkers gossiped about what the meeting could be about. Some speculated that there could be big raises coming, while others thought it was simply a meeting for the company to brag about their end-of-year profits. Decka, of course, knew what was really going to be discussed at the meetings. Layoffs.

Friday arrived, and the entire staff found their way to the largest meeting room the building had. Although the room was very large, the associates needed to squish in to make room for everyone. There were five people dressed up in suits sitting at the front of the room. While unfamiliar to most, it was evident that these individuals were 'big wigs' within the company.

"Thank you all for coming today and taking your time out from your busy days," one of the suits announced in a manner to let everyone know the meeting was starting. Decka thought it was strange that he thanked the staff for coming, considering nobody was given a choice *not* to attend.

The man introduced himself and his title, 'Vice President of Operations.' Decka didn't think it was important enough to remember the name he introduced himself with or the names of the other people he pointed out on the panel. He probably should have said, "Hi, everyone, we're upper management," and that would have sufficed.

A few moments later, he got to the point of the meeting. "As a company, we have made some tough decisions to stay competitive with the market," he said solemnly.

Decka knew what was coming. He tensed in his seat.

"Which is why, at the end of February, we will be moving this site's day-to-day operations overseas." The VP's words hung heavy in the air.

The news hit with a deafening silence. With just one sentence, Mr. Vice President of Operations had crushed everyone's soul.

One of the other upper management minions chimed in, attempting to soften the blow, "I know this is hard to hear, but we will be working with you to offer a smooth transition out and a severance package." The lady who was now talking seemed just as insincere as the first guy.

"We are going to show a PowerPoint and a timeline that should make things clearer and hopefully ease this news," she continued, grabbing a clicker. She turned on a presentation she thought was going to make people feel better. Most people had started to look toward each other to find some kind of solace. Decka understood what they must have been feeling, since he had learned about the news only a couple of months back.

The presentation was mind-numbing and tried to make a positive case economically why the company had to move this part of the company overseas. Without even seeing it, everyone knew what the reason was. Pure greed!

The presentation was almost over when the Human Resources suit took over his part. This was the part Decka should have closed his eyes and ears for. It only took a couple of bullet points before he blew his top, unable to contain himself any longer.

"So, for the severance to work, you will need to train your assigned overseas counterpart until the doors close here on February twenty-eighth," the HR rep stated matter-of-factly.

Decka couldn't take it anymore. He shot up from his seat. "Wait, excuse me?!" he exclaimed.

The Vice President noticed the presenter wasn't finished and attempted to calm Decka. "I'm sorry, we will take questions at the end here."

But Decka didn't care. "I have a question now," he said defiantly.

"Derek, please wait until the end," the VP implored.

Decka looked around and saw Edna trying to calm the situation, shaking her head pleadingly.

He was not convinced to keep quiet. "Are you telling us, that we have to train our replacements, or we don't get paid out severance?" he demanded, voice rising.

The lady in the suit responded, "Well, it's our way of ensuring our customers get the same great service they deserve."

"They deserve?" Decka questioned emphatically. "What about what we deserve?"

"Derek, please?" Edna practically begged.

But he was just getting started. "Do you know how hard these people work and deserve these jobs? Do you know that some of these people were near retirement and probably thought they were set for life?"

"DEREK!" Edna pleaded again, louder this time.

He stopped and stared at her for a moment. "Why are you defending them? You don't even have a job after February, either."

Turning back to the panel of suits. "Let me guess," he said, his voice dripping with sarcasm, "you all made yourselves feel less guilty by waiting to fire us until after Christmas. As if dragging it out a few extra weeks would somehow make you the good guys, even though you've known about this since at least last November."

"Well, what about people who celebrate life every day?" he continued ranting. "Did you consider that your crappy severance and unemployment are not going to pay us what we make in full? That some here might not be able to put food on their tables or keep a roof over their heads?"

He paused, glaring at them. "And for what? For greed?"

Decka stood up and headed towards the door, fists clenched.

"Derek, I don't think you'll get the severance if you walk out that door," Edna called out desperately.

He stopped and spun around. "You can shove the severance and this job!" Then, saying something he'd wanted to for some time, he declared firmly, "By the way, my name is Decka!"

He knew that it left everyone confused, but just the fact he said it loud and proud, felt so freeing!

Decka grabbed his keys and drove away from the place he had worked for a long time, for the last time. He was only a few miles down the road when he realized his financial situation was now more dire. He walked into his house five hours earlier than expected, which was a surprise for everyone.

"Is everything okay, Good Buddy?" asked Bill.

Decka explained to Bill what happened.

"Are we going to need to go into storage if we can't stay here?"

"I won't let that happen," Decka assured him.

"I'm going to find a job, and we'll be okay just like we always are," he added. "At least we'll all be able to spend more time doing Christmassy things for the next few weeks."

He opened his laptop and started searching for job opportunities, but there didn't seem to be much available. The positions he came across were either beyond his level of experience or offered low pay. Despite feeling underpaid at the job he just walked out on, he hesitated to quit; after all, it still provided more income than the opportunities he was seeing.

Alicia and Barney stopped by later that day, and he told her what had happened. She offered some advice and suggested he should update his resume. He thought that was great advice and spent the rest of the evening revamping it. The next day, he spent all day applying for any job he thought might hire him.

The days passed, and not one call came to ask for an interview. The only thing that came in which he once again didn't see, was a notice from the bank telling him he missed another mortgage payment. That was the second notice.

A few more weeks passed, and there was no calls or emails from any of the jobs Decka applied to. He made an appointment with a hiring agency in the hopes they could help him find something. They informed him that it was a tough time in the economy, and a lot of companies weren't hiring. Decka wasn't sure if that was true or if they were just giving him the runaround. Either way, it wasn't helpful. His hopes and money were dwindling fast, and he was starting to be stressed.

Decka sat around the house and waited for anyone to call him for a job. One night, Alicia came over and accidentally bumped into the stack of letters that had been built up on the kitchen counter. The one envelope that slid the furthest was from the bank, which had in big black letters: IMPORTANT: LATE PAYMENT SECOND REQUEST.

Alicia saw it and said, "Oh no, this isn't good." She handed the letter to Decka.

"Oh, I'm sure it's just the mortgage company complaining about their payment," he said dismissively. "It's not like I didn't pay them anything. I paid what I could, which is something at least."

Alicia's brow furrowed with concern. "They are sticklers, though, and don't care." She shook her head. "Unfortunately, it's all you could afford to send them."

She glanced at the calendar. "It's almost time for another monthly payment too, probably."

"Yeah, I'm sure any day now, the mailperson will deliver another reminder," Decka said, his voice heavy with dejection.

Alicia sat down at the table in front of Decka. "What if you moved in with me?"

Decka sat there in silence, stunned by her bittersweet suggestion. He knew he couldn't do it without sacrificing everyone else in the house. How could he even say no? How could he explain why he had to refuse?

"Say something?" Alicia prompted, her expression growing concerned.

"I don't know how to say this, but I can't," he finally answered, unable to meet her gaze.

Her face fell, sadness etching her features. "I know it's a huge move, but it could help save money."

"It's not that," Decka replied, shaking his head.

Confusion crept into Alicia's voice. "Well, if it's not about saving money or avoiding filing for bankruptcy, what other reason is there?"

Decka's throat tightened, feeling cornered. "I can't tell you."

Her brow creased as she fought to understand. "I don't get it. You're probably only one missed payment away from losing everything."

"I just can't tell you," He reiterated, his tone edged with frustration.

"Well, if you can't say, then it must be me?" she suggested, doubt lacing her words.

"It's definitely not you," Decka insisted, his voice rising slightly.

Alicia's voice rose to match his. "Well, it's got to be me, and you don't want to live with me."

"That's really, really not it," he countered, his voice growing louder too.

"Apparently, you're too scared to tell me that it's me, because unless you come into money within the next few weeks, you probably can't stay here," she argued, her volume escalating.

Unable to contain himself any longer, Decka finally yelled, "I CAN'T TELL YOU BECAUSE YOU WON'T BELIEVE ME!"

Alicia's eyes flashed with determination. "WELL, IF YOU CARE ABOUT ME AT ALL, YOU'LL TRY ME!"

Decka's expression softened, his voice thick with emotion. "CARE ABOUT YOU? I AM IN COMPLETE LOVE WITH YOU, ALICIA!"

Her brow knitted in frustration. "WELL, IF YOU LOVE SOMEONE, YOU DON'T TELL THEM THAT YOU CAN'T TELL THEM SOMETHING, DEREK!"

Realizing there was no other option, Decka relented. "FINE, YOU WANT TO HEAR WHY?"

"YES!" Alicia insisted, her hands balling into fists.

"WELL, REMEMBER THAT NIGHT I GOT DRUNK AND TOLD YOU MY NAME WAS DECKA?"

"YES!" Alicia answered.

"WELL, MY NAME *IS* DECKA, AT LEAST THE NAME I WANT TO BE CALLED BY!"

Alicia's expression shifted to one of bewilderment. "WOW, ARE YOU DRUNK RIGHT NOW?"

"NOPE, DRY AS COULD BE," Decka affirmed. "AND REMEMBER I TOLD YOU SCARF MADE COFFEE?"

Exasperation crept into her voice. "HOW COULD I FORGET?"

"WELL, HE IS REAL AND ALIVE," Decka pressed on, his voice ringing with conviction.

"OH, BOY," Alicia muttered, rolling her eyes.

"AND SO IS BILL, RAYNE, DEAR, SUPERMAN, FRASER, THE ANGEL ON TOP OF FRASER, AND ALL THE OTHER DECORATIONS IN THE HOUSE!"

Lowering her voice out of sheer exhaustion, Alicia asked, "Why are you doing this?"

He lowered his voice too, his tone earnestly. "I'm not making this up. See? I knew you wouldn't believe me!"

Her frustration fading, replaced by a weary curiosity, she said, "I can't believe I'm going to ask this." She hesitated, then continued, "How are they alive (using her fingers to mimic air quotes), and why can't I see them?"

Decka's shoulders sagged with relief, grateful for her willingness to hear him out. "It's a long story, and I don't even understand it all, but it has something to do with Christmas magic."

Alicia's brow arched skeptically. "Christmas magic?"

"Yeah, and for some reason, only I can see and hear them, and that also has something to do with the Christmas spirit I have inside me."

Her tone dripped with sarcasm as she said, "Wow, this is getting good."

Sensing her doubt, Decka sighed. "Okay, fine, this is again why I never told you."

To his surprise, Alicia's expression softened. "I want to hear more, please."

"Last Fourth of July, when I ran in to get ice for Jerry's party, I heard them singing up in the attic." Decka tried to explain.

"Let me guess, they were singing 'Rocking Around the Christmas Tree'?" Alicia quipped with sarcasm.

"Actually, it was 'Cruel Summer,'" Decka replied matter-of-factly.

"Why then?" Alicia pressed; her curiosity piqued.

"Well, I think I surprised them, and they said they never wanted to interfere because my life was stressful already."

Understanding lit up on Alicia's face. "Like now?"

"Exactly, like now," Decka confirmed with a somber nod.

A flicker of skepticism returned to Alicia's features. "I must admit, I'm impressed you thought of all of this on the fly right now instead of just telling me you don't want to move in with me and would rather risk being homeless."

Decka shook his head vehemently. "That's not it." He paused, gathering his thoughts. "If I move somewhere else, I'd most likely have to put them in storage for the time being, and I can't do that to them."

Alicia's brow furrowed as she attempted to make sense of his words. "So, let me get this straight: only you can see these haunted Christmas decorations because you have Christmas spirit?"

"They're not haunted; they're alive and take the image of whatever they want to be," Decka corrected gently.

"So, I like Christmas; why can't I see them?" Alicia challenged.

Decka took a deep breath, trying his best to explain. "It's great that you like Christmas, but it's something you have to truly believe in, just without the decision to believe. It's got to be automatic."

Alicia considered his words for a moment. "Well, is there anything more?"

"Yes," Decka affirmed. "My Christmas spirit and magic let me be and see myself as what I feel and want to be, too."

Her brow arched quizzically. "And what kind of decoration are you?"

Bracing himself, Decka admitted, "I'm actually, eight years old again."

Alicia's eyes widened in disbelief. "What?"

Decka held her gaze steadily. "When I look in the mirror and how they see me, it is as an eight-year-old."

Shaking her head, Alicia turned around and headed towards the door. "Now, I've heard everything."

"Where are you going?" Decka called after her, concern lacing his voice.

"I can't take this ridiculousness," she tossed over her shoulder.

"But it's true," Decka insisted, following her down the driveway.

"Please stop, Alicia."

She kept walking, her voice tinged with sadness. "I'm going home to Barney. At least he's real."

Decka pointed toward the front of the house, his voice edged with desperation. "How do you think I put all those lights up so fast?" He swallowed hard before continuing, "Did you really think I could have done that overnight by myself?"

Alicia's lips curved into a bitter smile as she replied with dripping sarcasm, "No, it must have been the magical Christmas decorations."

"That's exactly how it happened!" Decka insisted, still trying to convince her despite the sarcasm lacing her words.

But Alicia had reached her limit. Tears welled in her eyes as she shook her head. "See ya later, Derek or Decka or whatever your name is." She turned and started walking away, her shoulders trembling with suppressed sobs.

Decka's heart clenched as he watched her crying figure retreat. He couldn't bear to see her so distraught and realized the best thing was to let her go home for now. He stood rooted to the spot, silently watching her disappear down the sidewalk, wondering if this was the last time he'd see her.

With a heavy heart, Decka walked back into the house to find everyone waiting in the kitchen, their expressions mirroring his own sadness.

"This is all our fault," Rayne said, hanging his head in shame.

Dear spoke up tentatively, "Maybe we should all go live back up in the attic?"

But Decka shook his head, resolute. "You're not going back in the attic or anywhere." He glanced out the window, his eyes haunted. "I just need to find a decent-paying job, and everything can go back to normal." He tried to sound convincing, but the hollowness in his voice betrayed the fact that he was rapidly losing all hope.

February came and Decka hadn't talked to Alicia in a couple of weeks. He didn't even see her walking Barney. He assumed she just went in another direction to avoid him altogether. He had gone from seeing her every day, to not at all. It was the worst Decka could ever remember feeling. He kept wondering if he could have thought of another lie, but knew it would have had to eventually come out.

He kept applying for jobs, but nobody called back. He barely had any money left with only enough for food and gas. The gas was simply in hopes that he would get a call to have to drive to an interview. The call never came.

It was a Wednesday afternoon when there was a knock at the door. He opened the door where his mail carrier was waiting.

"Sir, I have some certified mail that I need you to sign for."

Decka signed the green certified slip that the mail carrier handed to him and in exchange, was handed the letter. It was from the mortgage company. Without opening it, he knew what it most likely was. He walked into the kitchen, sat down at the kitchen table, and opened the letter. He scanned it at first, and somehow, the relevant information popped out immediately. His fear of what was inside the letter had come true. In just a quick scan, he understood completely what he was being informed of. Due to his missed third payment, the foreclosure process had begun. He had only thirty days to either pay what he owed, or vacate the home.

His heart fell into his chest. Decka looked at Bill, Scarf, Rayne, Dear, and everyone else who was silently staring in his direction and said, "I'm sorry."

Nobody said anything.

Over the next couple of days, Decka applied for even more jobs, hoping a miracle would occur. Nothing. He started looking for apartments that might allow him to rent, but with his bad credit, no landlord would accept his application. Even if he had, he wasn't sure he could come up with the first and last month's rent that was usually required. He was coming to the realization that he may have to live in his car until he got back on his feet. As terrible as that felt, he felt even worse that he was going to need to put his friends in storage. Decka didn't know how he could even tell them, after he promised he would never let that happen.

Decka pulled into his driveway and Jerry was standing outside.

"Hey, D-Man, I know you and something doesn't seem right." Jerry said. "What's been going on here?"

Decka explained everything to him. Well, about his job and the foreclosure. Not about the decorations. Jerry offered to loan him money, but Decka was too proud and thought of it as a handout. He thanked Jerry for the offer but told him he needed to find his way out of it. Jerry understood his position and told him that if he changed his mind the offer was always there. Decka was grateful for having such a good friend. Jerry asked about Alicia, and without explaining that Alicia didn't believe he talked to living Christmas decorations, Decka instead told him that they had just decided to go their own ways and that it wasn't meant to be. Jerry was shocked because it seemed to be going so well. Of course it had been.

Days passed, and time was running out. Decka still hadn't mentioned putting anyone in storage. He didn't think there was a point in making everyone sadder than they already were. He still prayed he could find a way to make the money needed to stay in the house or at least a place to stay where everyone could be free.

February ended and March began with Decka's luck still not improving. With no job leads, every phone call or mail delivery filled him with dread, unsure of what news they might bring.

Days passed without any significant developments, until a knock on the door brought everything he had been fearing.

KNOCK, KNOCK, KNOCK!

It sounded more like someone was using a sledgehammer. Decka and everyone whipped their heads around.

Decka peeked out the window and saw a police vehicle parked out front. He knew he couldn't ignore the knocking, so he opened the front door.

"Hello, sir, my name is Sheriff Logan from the county. Are you the owner?" the woman in uniform asked.

"I am," Decka answered.

"I'm sorry to inform you that the bank has purchased the deed for this property, and I am hereby required to issue this notice to vacate the premise within ten days."

She handed Decka a paper that had a seal on it and looked official. Either way, it's not like he had any defense and could fight it.

"I understand," he quietly said, looking down.

Sheriff Logan could tell Decka was depressed and down on his luck. "Sir, can I come in for just a moment?"

"Sure, it's not like it was my house anyway," Decka replied, but immediately regretted his words. "Sorry, Sheriff, I didn't mean for it to come out like that. "Decka stepped aside as a sign and invitation for her to come in. She was immediately surprised at all the Christmas decorations displayed all over. Not wanting to get into it, he said, "Don't mind it, I just haven't had the time to take it all down yet."

"It's all so beautiful." The sheriff was amazed, as she took in the situation. She took her hat off and sat down on the edge of a recliner. "It's not my place to say, and I don't know your circumstances, but if you don't have a place to stay, I've worked with a nearby shelter for over ten years. If you need help transitioning, it could be a good place to start."

Decka thought it was nice of the sheriff to offer help, and considering he might not have any other options, he realized he might have to seriously consider it. As the conversation was happening, he realized that everyone was just hearing the same thing that he was hearing.

They were being evicted.

13
Candy Cane Ville

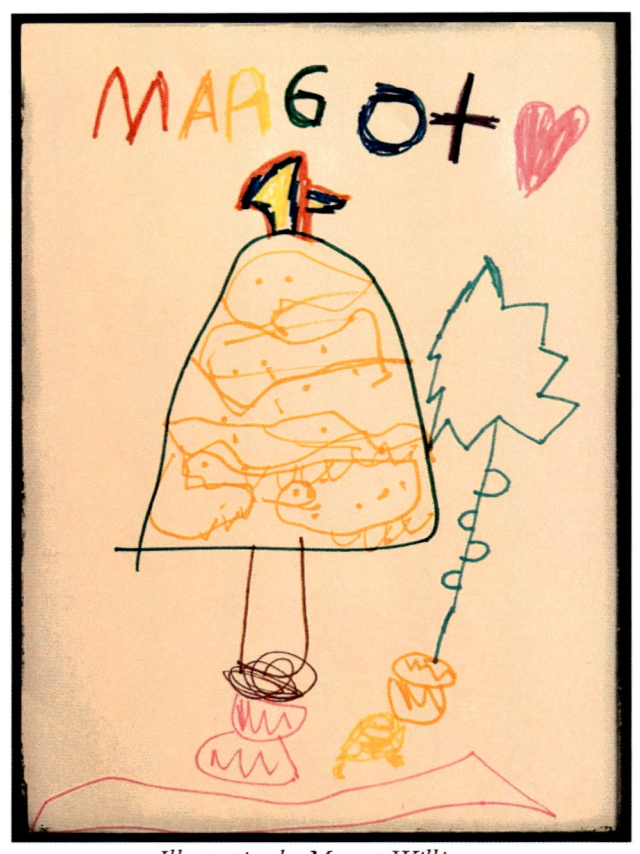

Illustration by Margot Williams

Decka thanked Sheriff Logan for her kind words and advice. Accepting his gratitude, she adjusted her cap and retrieved her business card, which she handed to him for future reference. As she made her way toward the front door to leave, the side door burst open. Alicia rushed in, accompanied by Barney, who unleashed a barrage of aggressive barks towards Sheriff Logan. Alicia struggled to control Barney; he strained against his leash with such force that it seemed he might snap it at any moment.

"BARNEY!" Alicia's voice rang out, laced with urgency. "Calm down!"

Despite her efforts, Barney's barking persisted, drowning out Alicia's attempts to explain.

Decka could barely make out what she had said with the piercing barking that was still happening.

Decka turned toward Sheriff Logan. "She's right. He's the sweetest dog and never acts like this."

"It's really okay. It's probably the uniform," Sheriff Logan said. "I'm pretty used to it."

"Well, I'll be on my way, and again, I'm sorry, but please call if you need assistance." Her hand was still on the doorknob, but this time turned it and walked out the front door.

Decka looked at Alicia and said, "Thank you for checking on me. I know I'm probably not your favorite person in the world."

"I still don't get it, but I still care," she said while unhooking Barney's leash. "I'm sorry for the chaos. I don't know what got into him."

Before Alicia could fully remove the leash, Barney bolted toward the front window and started barking uncontrollably again. Sheriff Logan was just getting into her cruiser, and the mere sight of her upset Barney.

"BARNEY!" Alicia yelled louder.

Barney continued to race around the living room in frantic circles before returning to the window, still seething with rage.

"WHAT'S GOTTEN INTO YOU, BARNEY?" Alicia's voice rose in volume, echoing her bewilderment.

"It's not like he's never seen a police vehicle driving by before," she said, attempting to comprehend her dog's behavior.

Sheriff Logan was still in her vehicle, which seemed to bother Barney even further. It was almost like he wanted to make sure she never came back there again. He was still frantically pacing, barking, and increasingly going berserk. In one last attempt to give Sheriff Logan a piece of his mind, Barney ran all the way into the kitchen and back to the window at full speed, unintentionally sliding into Fraser.

With the full velocity he had picked up, Barney's force was so great that Fraser swayed back and started to tip over. Decka, who was a few feet away, dove as rapidly as he could to try and catch the tree from completely falling over. Extending one arm, he managed to grasp one of Fraser's branches, just enough to halt the impending tumble. His other arm quickly followed, gripping the trunk's middle and steadying the tree. It seemed disaster had been averted.

As Decka straightened Fraser, the angel suddenly slipped from the tree's highest point, plummeting to the floor with a deafening crash. Although Decka hadn't witnessed the angel's descent, the sound of shattering glass beneath his feet alerted him to the mishap. His eyes widened in surprise, and he instinctively glanced downward.

"Oh no!" Decka fell to his knees where the gold porcelain pieces scattered. "No, no, no... please, no!"

"I'm so sorry," Alicia said, knowing how much the angel meant to Decka and unsure of what else to say.

Barney immediately stopped barking and somehow knew he had done something bad. He lay in front of the pile and began to whimper.

"I'm very, very sorry," Alicia repeated.

Decka couldn't even hear her as he picked up a small piece of the angel. He looked up at Alicia, and his eyes filled with tears. It was as if a floodgate had burst open. Tears streamed down his cheeks like cascading waterfalls.

Alicia somehow could see through his tears that all the things he had told her many weeks ago were true. All the emotion pouring out of him was real. Somehow, she also started feeling what he was feeling. Her vision began to blur, as if she were peering through an underwater ocean. Tears streamed down her cheeks, mirroring his own. In that moment, she felt the depth of his love washing over her too. She could feel his love for Christmas.

Then, it happened!

Alicia looked up and noticed the tree was moving, staring down at Decka and the broken angel. She glanced around and saw all the decorations come to life. They moved toward the tree and gathered in a circle. She should have been scared, but she wasn't. They were all sad and concerned about the angel. This is what Decka had been talking about. It was astonishing and beautiful, but also sad now at the same time.

Alicia couldn't even speak. She was just taking it all in.

Decka looked at everyone. "I think we lost her."

Scarf reached out his stick arm and patted Decka on the back with his mitten. "No one is ever gone."

Barney was still whimpering and nuzzled his wet nose up to Decka. Bill waddled over and petted him with his wing. "You didn't mean to cause her to fall, pal!"

Dear and Rayne walked over on both sides of Alicia. Rayne put his head under Alicia's hand as a gesture of comfort. Dear looked at her and said, "We know it was an accident."

"Thank you for saying that," Alicia replied.

Decka sprang up on his feet and turned around in amazement. "You can see them?"

With still a few tears in her eyes, Alicia nodded. "Yes, I can see and hear everything."

"I'm so sorry I didn't believe you," Alicia said, her voice filled with remorse.

"I understand, trust me. You actually are a little quicker at believing it than I was," Decka said clearing the tears from his own eyes.

Rayne added, "Believing is the keyword, Alicia!"

"Yes, it is!" she agreed happily.

Barney whimpered again, with his head down on the floor. Scarf stood over the scattered porcelain glass. "She was so beautiful!"

"Yes, she was," Decka sighed softly. "And she can never be replaced."

They all huddled around, seeking solace in each other's presence.

Suddenly, the mail slot in the front door opened, and a bright gold envelope came flying through. Like a feather, it swayed back and forth onto the floor near everyone's feet that was still gathered near Fraser. It landed face-up with letters written on it.

Rayne, closest to the fallen angel, bent his head down to inspect what was written in white glitter. After a moment, he looked up. "It says 'To Decka.'"

"You better open it, Good Buddy!" Bill suggested.

Decka picked the envelope up and opened it very carefully. Inside, he pulled out a wooden scroll that was rolled up tightly. He didn't open it at first. He inspected it from all angles because it seemed way too big to fit inside the envelope. He looked at everyone and asked, "How is that possible?"

Everyone just shrugged their shoulders. "Open it, Decka!" Scarf said.

He slowly unrolled the scroll, which unveiled vintage papyrus paper. The kind you might think a pirate's treasure map would be on. Decka read the perfectly cursive lettering. He didn't say anything, but he looked back down at the fragmented pieces of Angel on the floor.

"Well, what does it say?" Scarf was hopping up and down on the floor with curiosity.

Decka looked at Alicia, and then everyone else. "It says, 'Decka, there is no need to replace her.'" He paused with a look of confusion.

He looked back at the letter and read the last part out loud, almost as a question. "Bring her to Candy Cane Ville?"

He turned over the letter to see if there was a name on it. Then he turned it back to the written part of the letter to look again. "It doesn't say who it's from."

"Candy Cane Ville. I went there a bunch of times as a little girl," Alicia recalled with warm memories. "They had the best chocolate peppermint-covered apples."

She kept going, "And the best Christmas lights ever. The place is huge."

"Oh, and rides, so many rides. They have a roller coaster where the cars look like sleds, so when you're coming down the tracks that are white, you feel like you're actually on snow."

Alicia couldn't stop. "And then there's the Ferris wheel. It gets extra cold when you're at the top, because you know Candy Cane Ville is up in the mountains."

"But that's okay, because you can always have hot chocolate. They have a gigantic hot chocolate fountain that has the best hot chocolate around."

She paused for a second in thought. "Although, Decka, yours might have been the best hot chocolate now that I think about it."

"Actually, that was me," Scarf said, raising his stick arm.

Alicia didn't hear him. She continued happily rambling from where she had just left off. "There's also a gigantic General Country Store where you can buy the best handmade ornaments. One time, I bought the prettiest little gloves there. They had little light-blue snowflake patterns on them."

Decka had never experienced this side of Alicia before. Seeing the excitement on her face in everything she described and getting lost in the moment (even if it was years ago) moved him. As he watched her, he thought, "Just another reason I love her so much."

Alicia was still reminiscing and illuminating about the wonderful times at Candy Cane Ville. She was too engrossed in her thoughts to notice that everyone started staring at her with the widest grins on their faces.

"What are you all staring at?" she asked, curious. "Oh, I'm sorry I got lost in my thoughts there, didn't I?"

"Nope, not at all," Bill answered.

Decka seemed to be smiling a little extra wider than everyone. "Okay, are you ready for this one?"

"Ready for what?" Alicia replied.

Decka grabbed her by the hand and brought her over to a full-length mirror. "Okay, this one really awestruck me."

She stared at Decka and hadn't looked into the mirror yet. "Go ahead," he coaxed her into looking by extending his arm toward her image. Hesitantly, she slowly turned around.

"Holy smokes!" she shouted.

Alicia was eight years old. She whipped back toward Decka. She could now see him as an eight-year-old. And then she repeated herself.

"Holy smokes! You're little, too!"

Decka laughed. "Yeah, we're in the image that we feel. I guess all that talk about Candy Cane Ville made you feel like a little Alicia kid again."

She looked back at herself in the mirror and couldn't help but just start laughing out loud. "This is craaaaaaaaaaaazy!"

The phenomenon that occurred momentarily distracted everyone from the letter that was still in Decka's hand. The momentary forgetfulness passed the minute he looked back at the scroll in his hand. He looked at it again and then back toward the pile of glass on the floor under Fraser.

"What do we do?" Decka asked.

Alicia looked at him and spoke. "I think we need to take a ride to the mountains to Candy Cane Ville."

Decka walked back over to the pile and began picking up every little piece of the angel. "If we leave now, we can be there by tomorrow afternoon."

"I'll run home quick and grab some food and water for Barney, and we can leave right away," Alicia replied.

"I wish I had more room in my car for everyone, but unfortunately, I don't," Decka announced to everyone. "We'll be back in a few days and let you know what happens."

Decka carefully selected the fluffiest towel he could find and gently placed the pieces of the angel into it, ensuring that no fragments would be further broken or lost. With care, he softly wrapped the towel around the delicate pieces and secured them in a sturdy bag. By the time he was finished, Alicia had already made her way back. She was still amazed at her transformation inside and out.

"I don't get it; my clothes just seem to change size with me," she said in astonishment.

"Yeah, I'm not sure I've gotten used to that one myself," Decka replied, a blend of humor and honesty in his tone.

He grabbed his car keys and was about to walk out the door when he turned back around and said, "Well, at least you can stay up all night listening to Christmas music and watching holiday movies."

Alicia, Decka, and Barney walked down the driveway and were about to get in the car when they were alarmed by a loud car horn.

HONK, HONK, HOOOOOONK!

They all whipped their heads around and saw Jerry pulling in front of the house with a twenty-foot U-Haul moving truck. He shut the engine off and hopped out of the driver's side.

"What's that for Jerry?" Decka asked.

"Well, D-Man, I felt bad about everything, and I knew you wouldn't take any money, so I thought I could at least rent this for you and help you out a little with the moving and storage of your things."

"Oh man, you're the sweetest," he said thankfully.

"I felt I had to do something."

Looking at the truck, an idea shot into his head. "Jerry, I have no right to ask this, but would you be okay if, before I started packing it with boxes, I took it on a trip for a couple of days?"

"Do whatever you need to do, D-Man," Jerry responded with no hesitation. He flipped Decka the keys and headed back toward his house next door.

"Hey, Jerry!" Decka yelled. He handed Alicia the bag holding the angel and ran over to Jerry.

"Thanks," Decka said, giving a big hug.

"Anytime," Jerry replied, looking over at Alicia. "Glad to see you two seem to have worked things out."

"Oh yeah," Decka replied. "We definitely figured it out."

Jerry went into his house, and Decka walked back to Alicia, who was still in the driveway. "Okay, well, I think everybody can go now."

Looking down at the wrapped towel in the bag, Alicia asked, "Do we know if we have enough time?"

Decka laughed. "Oh yeah, we do!"

He unlocked the door he had just locked and walked back into the house and into the living room. Before saying anything, he leaned into Alicia's ear to whisper, "Wait until you see this."

Decka then stood up straight in a motion to make an announcement, "Okay, listen up, everyone." Just these words were enough for everyone to stop and listen. "We found a way for us all to go to Candy Cane Ville!"

Cheers erupted from everyone.

"Here's how this will work!" Decka thought for a moment and then spoke louder, "This goes for outside, too!"

"We have a big truck outside," he continued. "I will go out front and open the back roll-up door. I'll then make sure no one is coming up or down the street."

"When I yell, 'THE COAST IS CLEAR,'" Decka instructed, "everyone make their way into the vehicle. There should be enough room for everyone."

He looked at Fraser, thought for a moment that he was the only one who was a little slower and added one more stipulation. "One more thing. When I yell, 'THE COAST IS CLEAR,' let Fraser go first, and then everyone else follows."

Everyone agreed and waited for Decka to go outside and be on the lookout. Before he walked out the door, he whispered once again to Alicia.

"You might want to step aside for this one," he said, chuckling.

Decka went outside, opened the back of the U-Haul, and looked both ways for traffic. There was one car coming, and knew it would be clear after it passed. He held his arm up in preparation for waving, giving everyone the green light. The automobile passed and was quickly out of sight. One more check of the street and Decka yanked his arm down in a chop motion and yelled. "COAST IS CLEAR!"

In perfect synchronicity, every Christmas decoration started parading toward the door. Some were marching, and some were flying if they could. Some that were displayed higher up on shelves, were helped down by cardinals, turtle doves, and calling birds for purposes of speed. Superman helped untangle Fraser from all the lights and garland to get him free for his trip to the mountains. Even the choo-choo train under the tree was packed and neatly disassembled track by track with the help of every living ornament that had climbed down off the branches. Some even used garland to rappel themselves off Fraser.

As all this was occurring, Alicia looked all around admiring the harmony of it all. Fraser was the first one free, and like he did up in the attic to come down to the main level of the house, hopped around to the front door. He gave a quick look for Decka, who was still at the back of the U-Haul. He waved him and everyone on.

"COME ON, IT'S STILL CLEAR!" he reiterated.

Fraser made his way down the front steps and hopped onto the U-Haul ramp and into the very back of the truck. He was followed in perfect rows by everyone else who made their way down the stairs, almost like army soldiers. The last few who came signaling the end of the procession were Bill, Scarf, Rayne, and Dear.

They made their way into the U-Haul, and there was only the final wave to go. With one loud whistle, the decorations that were displayed outside hopped, walked, and flew themselves off of the house and into the U-Haul. Decka and Alicia checked in the back and admired how everyone arranged themselves to fit comfortably.

Alicia said, "It was like watching the most captivating three-ring circus performance, and it only took..." (looking at her watch) "...five minutes in total?"

Bill raised his wing and corrected her proudly, "Four minutes and thirty-four seconds, to be exact."

Decka closed the ramp and grasped the rope to lower the U-Haul door. "We should arrive by tomorrow afternoon."

Alicia hurried to the car where Barney patiently waited in the backseat. She gathered him and his leash, along with the bag containing the angel. Decka settled into the driver's seat as Alicia and Barney joined him in the passenger area.

Placing the bag beside her and Barney, Alicia noticed him sniffing it with a wet nose, emitting one more mournful puppy whine.

Decka turned the key and let out a little bit of a sigh himself when he looked at the radio.

"What's the matter?" Alicia asked.

"It's a long drive, and we can't listen to Christmas songs," Decka replied.

Bill yelled from the back, "Turn it to AM station 1225, Good Buddy!"

Decka pushed the bottom to switch the FM to AM and turned the dial to 1225. "It's Beginning to Look a Lot Like Christmas" started playing. Alicia and Decka looked at each other and smiled.

"Wait, was this station always there?" Decka yelled back to Bill.

"Yeah, sorry I forgot to tell you," Bill answered.

"Oh well." Decka shrugged his shoulders and asked one more question before putting the truck into drive. "Okay, everybody, know what time it is?"

"What?" a chorus of voices in the back asked.

"TIME FOR A ROAD TRIP!" Decka declared.

"YAAAAAY! A ROAD TRIIIIPP!" echoed a louder chorus from everyone in the back. Decka stepped on the gas, and they were all headed to Candy Cane Ville.

They drove the rest of the day and into the night, only stopping a few times for gas. Everyone sang every line of every Christmas song that came on the radio. It was very dark as they drove out of the various towns and into the mountains. Alicia and Decka took turns switching driving duties overnight to keep their eyes fresh as they made their way through the windy roads. It was mid-March, and there was still some snow on the ground the higher the elevations they reached. The morning had come, and soon they were again driving in the daylight. After one final fill-up and rest stop, Decka, Alicia, and Barney saw the first sign that let them know they were close.

It read: CANDY CANE VILLE 30 miles EXIT 10.

Decka was driving again and yelled, "WE'RE CLOSE, EVERYONE! WE'LL BE THERE IN LESS THAN AN HOUR!"

Another "YAAAAAY" erupted from the back of the U-Haul.

They saw two more signs for Candy Cane Ville as they cruised closer to Exit 10. They followed the sign to bear right off the exit and made their way down the two-lane highway for three miles until they reached the final sign they needed. A thirty-foot wooden Nutcracker soldier pointing to a road that read, "ENTRANCE."

As they turned onto the road, they drove for a quarter of a mile until they reached a closed metal gate. Decka pulled in slowly, rolling down the window to get a better view.

"I can see the parking lot is right on the other side of the gate, but how do we get in?" he asked out loud.

"Yeah, I can see through the gate too, but I don't see any cars like anyone is even here," Alicia said.

He then noticed a black pole on the driver's side close to where the gate would open. He inched up to the box and looked for any type of instructions. There weren't any keys, just a numeric pad with numbers to punch. Of course, they wouldn't know the security combination. He kept looking and somehow noticed there was a black button at the bottom of the box. It was just as black as the box itself, which is probably why he didn't see it. Maybe it was a doorbell or some kind of alert to somebody. It was worth a try, so he pushed it.

"What are the magic words?" a voice asked.

"Wait, what?" Decka asked, addressing the speaker.

The voice asked again, a little louder. It sounded like a child's voice speaking through a synthesizer. Decka wasn't sure if it was their actual voice or if the speaker at the gate was bad. He was able to make out what was being asked, though, but repeated it one more time just for clarity.

"Did you say, WHAT ARE THE MAGIC WORDS?"

"Yeah, you know, the magic words!" the voice asked, as if Decka should have known them.

Alicia's face lit up. "I know what they are!" She managed to shuffle herself over Barney and leaned just enough over Decka to get her head out the driver's side window. Facing the speaker, she proudly exclaimed the answer, "MERRY CHRISTMAS!"

The voice in the speaker replied festively, "MERRY CHRISTMAS TO YOU TOO!"

The metal gate flashed with electricity and now, seemingly powered, started to open. Alicia, Decka, and Barney looked at each other with excitement. As they watched the gate slowly sway open, they shouted to everyone in the back, 'WE MADE IT, AND WE'RE IN, EVERYBODY!'

That was the loudest cheer yet!"

14
Stars

Illustration by Audra Lozada

The gate to the park was fully open, signaling that Decka, Alicia, Barney, and everyone in the U-Haul were officially invited inside. They rolled forward slowly, passing through the gate. The parking lot, which moments ago had seemed deserted, now appeared more welcoming with its freshly paved surface and new white lines. Not a single piece of wind-blown trash could be seen on the ground. Decka still had his window cracked open and could hear Christmas music as they approached the park. Alicia rolled down her window to hear it better. As they drew closer, they began to hear the sounds of carnival rides, people laughing, and all the other noises typical of an amusement park.

"The park's open?" Alicia's eyebrows shot up in surprise.

"Definitely sounds like it," Decka replied, equally surprised.

Even though it sounded like the park was full of people, there weren't any cars in the parking lot, and they could easily see the ticket booth where they needed to go. They pulled into the first row closest to the entryway. Alicia handed the bag with the angel to Decka, then put the leash around Barney.

"We'll be right back!" Decka yelled to everyone in the back.

They hopped out of the U-Haul and walked over to the ticket counter. Just a few feet away, they were relieved to see someone attending the station. They reached the window and were greeted by a unique-looking individual.

"Welcome to Candy Cane Ville!" the person said with the same toned voice as what they just heard in the speaker outside the gate.

Alicia and Decka didn't mean to stare at the worker, but they had unusually huge pointy ears and a ski-sloped nose. The person at the booth noticed their obvious staring.

"Yes, I'm an elf!" they continued, "You're going to see tons of us working here today!"

Decka snapped out of his trance and spoke, "I'm really sorry. I didn't mean to."

The elf cut him off, "It's okay. We get it all the time! Now, what are you here to do today?"

Decka reached into his pocket and grabbed the letter and placed it on the counter. "Someone sent this to me and said to come here."

The elf looked at it and said, "Oh, you must be Decka."

"That's me!" Decka exclaimed. In his other hand, he raised the bag holding the angel and placed it on the counter. "We're actually here for her," Decka clarified. The elf looked at it with empathy. "Ahhhh, I understand!" he said, then continued, "Just go on in and head to Santa's Lodge."

There are maps everywhere to show you how to get there. Mr. K is waiting for you there."

"Thank you," Decka said.

He, Alicia, and Barney turned and took a few steps past the ticket booth, heading toward the park. The elf jumped off the stool on which he was sitting on and left the booth to stop them momentarily. They all became wide-eyed again when the elf's head met them at their waist. They didn't notice his three-foot body sitting on a stool. The elf pointed toward the U-Haul.

"They can come too. They're all safe here."

The trio wasn't sure how the elf knew the U-Haul was carrying cargo, but surprises were suddenly becoming normal. Decka hustled back to the truck, pulled out the ramp, and rolled up the back door.

"Okay, everyone, we can all go into the park!" he announced with glee.

Just like they had piled in back at home, the living decorations exited the trailer in an orderly manner and gathered at the entrance of Candy Cane Ville.

"Okay, everyone, lets go in and find Santa's Lodge!"

They walked under a big archway that read: "WELCOME TO CANDY CANE VILLE." Alicia and Decka laughed as they entered under one side as adults and came out as children.

"But of course," Alicia laughed, slowly getting used to the wonderment.

Making their way into the theme park, they were instantly amazed by the sights, smells, and sounds. Lights and decorations were endless. It was still daytime, and somehow, everything was bright and dazzled as if it was night. The air smelled like the most magnificent blend of cinnamon, nutmeg, and gingerbread. Christmas music and laughter provided the soundtrack for the sweetest things heard.

The pathway they entered branched into three different directions. Conveniently, there was a large map off to the side of the path that showed the layout of Candy Cane Ville. They stopped and looked at the overlay and found on the map where they were currently standing. They then needed to see where Santa's Lodge was and make their way there. Alicia spotted it clearly marked.

"This way!" she declared and started down the path that was most left. All followed like happy ducks in a row.

Following the path, they looked around and could see some of the rides in the distance. Hands were raised in the air on a near, but far-off roller coaster creaking over its first steep hill. A little to the right of it, they could see an even taller Ferris wheel turning slowly. Alicia pointed to it.

"That's the Ferris wheel I was talking about!" she shouted with excitement. They walked along, and a few elves passed them by. They laughed to themselves hearing their voices were identical with the same pitch and the same tone. There was something adorable about it. A few more paces and they spotted Santa's Lodge.

"Yup, now I remember this too!" Alicia said. "It looks exactly the same!"

It was a rectangular log cabin with a huge chimney that had smoke rising out of it. They made their way up the walkway that was marked on the sidelines with different-sized wrapped Christmas gifts. Each got bigger as you got to the steps of the door. By the time Decka, Alicia, and Barney reached the front door, Fraser, Bill, Scarf, Rayne, Dear, and everyone else had filled the entire length of the pathway. There was a gold knocker on the door. Decka reached for it.

TAP, TAP, TAP!

The door opened, and there she was standing in front of everyone. The lady who greeted them was unmistakable. Whether it was the red dress with white fluffy trim, or the white hair that was tucked under her bonnet, or the little round glasses that lay right above her rosy cheeks. There was no doubt it was Mrs. Claus.

Still, she introduced herself.

"Well, hi, everybody. I'm Mrs. Santa Claus! Come on in, my husband is waiting for you."

She noticed everyone else waiting down the walkway. "Oh my, I didn't know there would be so many of you," She giggled.

"Well, we can only take a few of you at a time because we don't have a lot of room in this old house here!"

Decka looked back, held up the broken angel in the bag, and said, "We'll take her in first, and then you can all take turns saying hi, okay?"

"We understand!" Scarf relayed.

Alicia, Decka, and Barney followed Mrs. Claus who brought them into a room that was just on the side of the door they walked in. They first noticed the huge fireplace that had been pumping out the chimney outside. A couple more steps, and there was the man in red. He wasn't fully dressed in his entire red suit, but he had red pants and big black boots on. His top was a white union suit with gray suspenders overlaying them. He wasn't wearing his hat which only highlighted his snowy white hair and even fluffier, curly white beard. He was reading a book which he put down as soon as his guests had arrived. Alicia and Decka should have been star-struck but somehow felt perfectly comfortable. Decka for sure knew he had met Santa years ago, and Alicia just figured she did but couldn't remember when.

"Santa stood up from the leather chair he had been sitting in. 'Well, hello, Decka, Alicia,' he said, looking down, 'and Barney!'"

He walked over and patted Barney on the head, who started wagging his tail in joy.

"So, glad you made it here safely!" he said.

"Thank you for the letter!" Decka replied.

"I would have met you at your house, but I stopped here for a little visit, and I thought to myself: I think Alicia, Decka, and Barney would love this place!"

"We were surprised it would be open this time of year!"

Santa chuckled as his suspenders moved in and out with his dancing belly. "For us True Believers, it's open all year 'round."

He continued, "And so are all the other Christmas parks in every state and every province around the world!"

"So, you don't just live at the North Pole?" Alicia asked.

"Well, I live there, and that's where all the toys are made," he went on. "But thousands of years ago, the elves built underground tunnels that connect all the parks. One little hop on a high-speed train, and just like that—" he snapped his fingers "—you're at whatever one you want to be at!"

Santa realized he was getting sidetracked and interrupted himself. He looked down at the bag Decka was holding and said, "Now, now, let me see her."

Decka handed the bag over to Santa, who gently grabbed it with his white glove. "Come follow me."

He walked over and opened a wooden door that was oval shaped at the top. They followed St. Nick through it, which led down a small hallway and eventually to another door.

"This is where my own little personal workshop is," Santa informed them. Then he looked back at them, with them following behind and put his finger over his lips. "Shhhhh...don't tell the elves about this; I don't like anyone messing with my tools!"

He somehow made himself laugh again with that comment as he opened the second door. His belly once again jiggled amusingly. At the back wall was a large wooden bench. Santa placed the bag on the table and carefully unwrapped the towel. Now completely unrolled, he looked at the sea of broken glass that lay before him. He scratched his beard and seemed to be thinking to himself. As Santa pondered his thoughts, Decka and Alicia noticed that there weren't any tools on or around the workbench. As a matter of fact, the only other thing in this room was the workbench.

"Ahhhh, I got it!" Santa said, pointing his finger in the air.

There was a small door on the upright part of the workbench. Santa opened it to reveal a tiny bottle that contained a glowing yellow sparkling dust. The size of the bottle was as small as the size of a baby's palm.

Santa unscrewed the cap and was about to pour the substance on the glass pieces but suddenly stopped. He looked at Decka, Alicia, and Barney and said with bliss, "Just so you know. She was never gone. One's Christmas spirit is never ever gone!"

Then he let out a big "HO! HO! HO!"

He looked back at the broken angel and poured the bottle of yellow sparkling dust onto the broken pieces. Although the tiny bottle should have been empty within seconds, it kept pouring and pouring and pouring. It seemed like there was an endless amount in the container.

Mystically, the pieces on the table began swaying from side to side. Then they started shaking. Soon, they were wiggling and, even sooner, started spinning. Santa took a step back as they rose up and hovered about the workbench. Mesmerized, Decka, Alicia, and Barney then watched the broken pieces crisscross each other in the air. They observed as each piece found its specific spot, waiting for the next piece to locate the place it needed to go.

When all the broken pieces found their location, they moved toward each other and reassembled the angel into perfect shape. For a quick glimpse, you could see the cracks where she broke. However, a yellow burst of light flashed over her, and in a blink, she was back together and looked brand new. The Angel flapped her wings with appreciation and flew circles around the top of the room.

Decka and Alicia were breath taken and couldn't say anything yet. Barney started jumping and barking with uncontrollable happiness

Santa petted Barney's head. "Eaaaasy boy! That's what got you in trouble in the first place!" Santa and his belly giggled again.

Decka thought about everyone still waiting outside. "We have to tell everybody!"

"You know the way!" Kris Kringle agreed, motioning to lead the way.

The front door opened, and before anyone else could walk through, Angel flew out and above everyone to a round of cheers and hugs.

Decka and Alicia turned toward Santa and Mrs. Claus, who joined in the front on the stairs. "Thank you so much."

Decka looked at Alicia and said, "Well, I guess we should make the trip back home."

"It's going to be very dark here soon. How about spending the rest of the day here?" Mrs. Claus said.

"Yes, yes!" Santa continued. "You can enjoy the park all day and get a good night's sleep in the Tinsel Town."

"Thank you for the offer, but honestly, we have just enough money to get home," Decka replied.

St. Nick's belly rolled as he laughed. "Well, lucky for you guys, everything is free here today."

"Really?" Alicia asked.

"Absolutely!"

With the biggest smile and hope on her face, she looked at Decka. He was grinning, too. With appreciation, he said, "How could we say no, Mrs. Claus?" Then she looked at everyone still filling up the walkway. "Actually, I'll tell them you'll need a few rooms."

Santa spoke up, "I just ask one favor?"

"Of course," Decka replied.

"Please come by in the morning before you leave!"

"Absolutely, Santa."

Alicia turned back down the stairs and chanted, "Okay, let's gooooo!"

She was so excited to go enjoy the rest of Candy Cane Ville and couldn't wait. Leading the way, she seemed to know where she was going. It was easy to follow her with all her excitement.

They spent the rest of the day enjoying the park, riding all the rides, indulging in Christmas treats, and visiting as many shops as possible. Bill, Scarf, Rayne, and Dear, along with all the other decorations, loved seeing and meeting their counterparts scattered throughout the park. They all talked to each other as if they were old friends. There were a few additional exhibits in the park that even Alicia didn't remember. One that ended up being one of Decka's favorites was a petting zoo, which was funny to him, because the only animals to pet were reindeer.

Occasionally, Decka and Alicia met other children roughly around their age. Decka asked one other eight-year-old how it was that nobody knew Candy Cane Ville was open.

"Here, it works like home," the boy explained. "If they don't feel the Christmas spirit, they can't see it."

He went on, "The only reason they can see it around November or December is that's the only time they allow themselves to feel it."

Alicia wondered about the parking lot. "Okay, but where are all the cars for all of those of us who believe all year round?"

The boy just laughed. "We just don't need them anymore."

Decka and Alicia thought that was a confusing answer but left it at that.

Hours and hours in Candy Cane Ville flew by in what seemed only minutes. They didn't even make it through half of what the park had to offer. It was late and everyone had gotten extremely tired. They all agreed it was time to make their way to Tinsel Town for sleep. At least they would leave in the morning well rested.

The following morning came, and after an overindulgent breakfast of pancakes and waffles covered in sprinkles and syrup, it was time to leave. Before they made the voyage back home, they needed to stop by and see Santa one more time.

As they did the afternoon before, they knocked on the door at Santa's Lodge. This time, Santa opened the door and stepped outside and in between Decka and Alicia. He put each arm around their shoulders and turned them around, facing everyone once again lined up on the walkway.

"Well, how was yesterday?" Santa asked.

"It was so awesome!" Alicia answered.

"Yeah," Decka added. "I love that petting zoo!"

"Ho! Ho! Ho!" Santa responded. "That was Mrs. Claus's idea."

The man in red looked down the walkway at everyone.

"So, what would you think about staying here?"

Everyone fell silent at the question.

"Like forever?" Bill asked.

"We have plenty of room!" Santa confirmed.

Decka could see the hope in the eyes of everyone. He thought about the offer for a moment. For the last couple of days, he almost forgot about the foreclosure on his house. But that nightmare was waiting for him when he got back home. In his heart, he knew immediately how much he would miss them but probably could visit occasionally. It seemed like an easy choice, but they needed to make sure it was a decision they would be okay with.

"I would miss you all, but it's better than having to put you in storage," He looked out at Candy Cane Ville, which seemed even larger in the morning sun. "You'll have so much more room to live and do things here."

Alicia grabbed Decka's hand, knowing how hard it was for him to let them go.

With a big rolling laugh, Santa looked back at Decka and Alicia and down to Barney and said, "I'm asking aaaaall of you!"

"Us?" Decka asked in surprise.

"Yes, you too!" he continued. "I know all about the house and your money troubles."

He took his arms off Decka and Alicia's shoulders, extended them out wide, and spun around. "Here at Candy Cane Ville or any park you want to visit, you don't need money!"

Thinking out loud, Alicia said, "You know we never did get to see where the underground tunnels were."

Decka was still curious about a few things. "Can we still visit our friends once in a while?"

"Of course," Santa replied, "we use Lift, which is different from the Lyft, L-Y-F-T."

"Okay, because we would need to visit our friends sometimes," Decka clarified.

"I understand," Santa affirmed.

"Oh wait, like Jerry." Decka thought about the truck out front. "We have to get the U-Haul back to him."

Santa put his hand on Decka's shoulder, looked at his face and smiled. "Do you remember when I saw you at the mall and told you to look up at the sky?"

Decka never forgot.

He felt ashamed telling Santa the truth about that night. "Santa, I'm really so sorry I fell asleep and I never got to see it."

St. Nick quietly chuckled, followed by a low-pitched "Ho, Ho, Ho!"

"I know, it's quite all right," Santa replied with a jolly smile.

"I can't believe I missed it," Decka responded, his brow furrowed in confusion.

"You didn't miss it at all," Santa assured him, his eyes twinkling.

"I didn't?" Decka asked, tilting his head quizzically.

"Nope," Santa shook his head.

"I don't understand," Decka said, spreading his hands in a questioning gesture.

"I just wanted you to keep looking up at the sky, Decka," St. Nick said, gazing upwards with a whimsical expression.

Santa continued, his voice taking on a mystical tone, "Ya see, there are stars up there, and some of those stars have Christmas Magic. Even me, Jolly 'Ole Nick, doesn't know how they do what they do."

"I just know that when you believe, whether you are born with it like you, or finally feel it like you," he said, looking warmly at Alicia. "Then, with Christmas in our hearts and souls, anything is possible," Santa explained, spreading his arms wide.

Decka understood and looked up at the twinkling sky. Then Santa finished with a gentle smile, "And you, Decka, always kept looking up at the sky. So, ya see, you didn't miss anything."

"So, I guess there's some Christmas magic in those stars to get the truck back to Jerry?" Decka asked, his eyes bright with hope.

"You got it!" Santa answered with a wink.

Looking at Alicia, Decka asked with a newfound determination, "What do we do?"

"Well, the bank is going to take your house," she said, her expression confident and resolute. "They can take mine too."

Decka shrugged his shoulders and proclaimed proudly, "WE'LL STAY!"

Everyone cheered and hugged in celebration! Frazer hopped up to Santa and gave him a big hug with his big branch arms, muttering in the deepest baritone voice, "This is the best day ever!"

Alicia laughed heartily, "That's the first time I've ever heard him speak."

"Me too!" Decka replied, chuckling.

"Santa, after all you've done, I have no right to ask for anything," Decka said, his expression one of gratitude. "But could I make a request for someone that really deserves it?"

"Of course, what is it?" Santa answered, his face open and welcoming.

After Decka whispered his request into Santa's ear, the jolly man straightened up, a broad, conspiratorial grin spreading across his face as if he relished the prospect of granting this special wish.

"I love it!" Santa exclaimed, confirming the request. Barney was sitting by Santa's big black boots, wagging his tail and poking Santa's knee with his wet nose. "And do you have a request too, Barney?"

"WOOF, WOOF, WOOF!" Barney leaped up and spun in the air.

Santa kneeled to Barney and stuck his neck out to listen. Barney put his wet nose in St. Nick's ear and licked it repeatedly. Another belly roll, and Santa stood up and looked down at the pup.

"HO! HO! HO! Consider it done, my furry friend!"

"Well, I'd better go in the house and help Mrs. Claus with the chores!"

He turned and headed back into the lodge. Before he closed the door, he turned back around one last time and said, "Merry Christmas to all and to all a GOOD DAY AND NIGHT!"

In unison and almost like they rehearsed, everyone replied, "MERRY CHRISTMAS SANTA!"

"Well, everybody, where are we going first today?" Alicia asked with glee. She was so happy she didn't even wait for a response and started striding down the pathways towards the park.

Decka caught up to Alicia, who was cheerfully strolling along. "I guess we should have asked if we stay at Tinsel Town every night."

Stopping in her tracks and scratching her head, Alicia admitted, "Oops, I guess we should have asked that."

Suddenly, there was a tap on Decka's shoulder. He turned around to find an elf reaching up to get his attention, speaking in the synthesized-sounding voice they'd heard from every elf.

"Santa wanted me to show you to your house and one other thing," the elf said. "Follow me."

He shuffled down the walking path in his striped green socks and red pointy shoes, and everyone followed. After about fifty yards, he turned down a single path that curved to an opening. He stopped and turned around before they could see around the bend. The elf pointed his finger and stepped aside to let them see around the bend.

The elf, beaming with a smile said, "Mr. K. asked us to build this for you to stay in."

They walked a few more steps to see around the turn that the house was the same exact house as back home. With eyes astounded and mouths open, Decka barely was able to ask, "Is this the same house?"

"Nah but built to an exact replica." the elf replied.

"I can't believe it," Alicia stated but then jokingly thought about what she said. "But I do believe it too!"

Decka looked at Bill, Scarf, Rayne, Dear, and everyone else and said, "Well, I guess you can all go in and make yourselves at home."

Like the marchers they were, they all made their way into the house by ground or by flight. Decka, Alicia, and Barney stayed out front with the elf.

"Thank you and all the other elves again," Alicia said with gratitude. "One of these days, you'll have to show us where that tunnel is so we can visit other parks."

That triggered something the elf also needed to tell them. "I almost forgot! The big guy told me to show you something else. Follow me!"

Just when they thought they'd seen everything, there was something else to see. The elf brought them to a part of Candy Cane Ville they hadn't been to yet. They arrived at a large circular brick building. They marveled at the architecture as they were ushered inside. There was a gigantic snow globe directly in the middle of the dome-shaped room. There was light snow swimming inside the glass orb. At first glance, they couldn't make out any objects in the middle like most common snow globes would have.

"Look closely," the elf instructed.

Alicia, Decka, and Barney edged closer, eager for a better view. It felt like the opening scene of a movie in a darkened cinema, a scene they knew all too well. Within moments, they recognized Jerry's house. The U-Haul sat in his driveway, unmistakable against the familiar backdrop. As the white screen side door swung open, Jerry emerged.

"Are we witnessing this live?" Decka turned to the elf, seeking confirmation.

The elf simply nodded.

Alicia caught the subtle expression on Decka's face. "Is this what you requested from Santa?"

"It is!" Decka exclaimed, snapping his head back to the scene unfolding before them. "I can't wait to see the look on his face."

Jerry walked over to the truck and noticed a gold letter that was stuck to the steering wheel. It was the same type that Decka had received a few days earlier.

He took out the scroll and read it out loud, "To Jerry. Thank you for everything. We know you love electronic gadgets. These should keep you entertained for a while. We'll see ya for your Fourth of July party! Merry Christmas, Love Derek—AKA Decka—Alicia, and Barney."

As they watched, it was evident that Jerry seemed perplexed. He looked at the letter again with a laugh and walked to the back of the U-Haul that had a gigantic red bow on it. Still baffled staring at a Christmas bow in March, he eventually rolled up the back door and was stunned to the point he dropped the letter. He put his hand over his mouth. The entire back of the trailer was filled with every kind of equipment or appliance he'd ever wanted: big screen TVs, stereo speakers, computers, a barbeque grill, a riding lawn mower, and various other gadgets he secretly wished for.

They watched for a few more minutes through the snow globe before realizing they should probably stop spying on him.

"We'll see ya soon, Jerry!" Decka said.

Alicia and Decka turned to leave when Barney started barking. They turned around, and Barney was obviously trying to get their attention.

"Oh yeah, we forgot Barney asked Santa for something, too," Alicia said.

They turned back and repositioned themselves in front of the glass. A house came on that they weren't familiar with. Alicia asked, "Do you know this house?"

Decka shook his head "No." A woman walked out her door holding a similar-looking scroll.

"Wait, is that Sheriff Logan?" Alicia asked.

Decka looked closer. "Yeah, it is!" They both looked down at Barney, who was panting with joy.

They could hear her read her letter too. "Dear Sheriff Logan. I'm sorry for barking at you crazy the other day. I was just trying to protect my friends! Please look in your backyard! From: Barney."

They watched Sheriff Logan walk into her backyard to see what was back there for her. She walked through her gate, and up ran a tiny puppy that was the same breed as Barney. She picked him up, and the puppy peppered her with kisses.

"Look, it's a baby Barney!" Alicia looked down and said, "Aww, buddy, that was very sweet of you."

"Yeah, I guess you deserve a big 'ole cinnamon pretzel today," Decka exclaimed.

That day and every day after became a merry mix of familiar traditions and new adventures. Some of the new Christmas adventures coming via the elf tunnels, they eventually found.

From time to time, they would embark on Lift sleigh rides to visit Jerry, Sheriff Logan, and other friends they missed. It always amused them to show up as adults, a stark contrast to the image of the eight-year-olds they mostly remained.

They made sure to visit Jerry on the 4th of July, a special tradition they wouldn't miss. Upon their return home, they would gather to sing a joyous rendition of "Cruel Summer," a tradition sparked by the wistful yet joyful memory of Decka hearing it sung by the Christmas decorations in his attic. Now, it was a happy rendition, a remembrance of that unforgettable and magical moment.

Decka and Alicia are middle aged and still stare up at stars searching for the slightest glimpse of Christmas magic. They always will believe. If there's more than believing, then that's them. It's an instinct. Kind of like breathing. The feeling of Christmas and everything that comes with it "Just Is."

AI image created by Derek Greenlee

A Note from the Author

Upon writing this book, I tried to capture the vision of Christmas that I hold dear. Like the characters in my story, I find myself thinking about Christmas multiple times throughout the year. My mother truly loved the holiday, and you might even consider our house cluttered with the number of decorations she put up. Yet, for all the effort she put into displaying them, she couldn't wait to box them all up and store away. I remember one year everything was down by December 26th. I never understood that.

As I've gotten older, I've noticed that fewer people care for the season. For many, it's become a hassle. I understand some of this sentiment. For example, some people work in retail and must endure excruciating hours to fulfill the demands of the "Edna's" of the world. I did it myself for over a decade and witnessed the chaos that the holidays can bring. Somehow, even during those times, I never lost the Spirit. It saddens me that the holiday cheer seems to be at an all-time low. I don't know if social media is to blame or just the faster-paced society we've become accustomed to. I hope this book brings a little of that warmth back into your hearts.

Although this story is fictional, I don't believe it truly is. There's a little bit of Scarf, Bill, Rayne, Dear, or Fraser in all of us. Maybe if we all just took a few moments to look up at the stars occasionally, we could at least momentarily forget about our troubles.

Speaking of stars, one of the highlights of this book is the illustrations preceding each chapter and the prologue. These illustrations were created by friends and family, whom I asked to draw scenes based on general descriptions of the chapters. The contributors, ranging from ages 6 to 60 and coming from diverse backgrounds, had no knowledge of the story's context, allowing their imaginations to take the lead. This unique approach was my way of seeing how others might visualize the scenes without knowing the full story. I hope these illustrations bring a special touch to "Cruel Summer." Each piece of art is dear to my heart, as unique and varied as the bulbs on a Christmas tree.

The cover was drawn by a person who means a lot to me and who was equally significant to this story. She sat with me for a while, asking detailed questions I wouldn't have even considered. With her attention to the smallest things, she somehow created exactly what was in my head—something I could never have drawn myself. Thank you, Kassie!

Lastly, although the scenes and events are fantasy, the feelings are real. This is especially true for everything involving Alicia. My wife's name really is Alicia, and I love her as much as Decka loves Alicia in this book—actually, even more! I wouldn't ever want to spend a Christmas or any other day without her. She is my belief system for everything good.

Feel free to wish anyone a Merry Christmas, no matter time of year or their beliefs. Your message is simply a hope for them to have a good day. You never know – you might just brighten someone's day with a smile!

Merry Christmas!
Derek Greenlee

Made in the USA
Columbia, SC
10 August 2024